FATAL FORTUNE

BLACKMOORE SISTERS COZY MYSTERY SERIES
BOOK 8

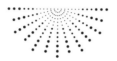

LEIGHANN DOBBS

This is a work of fiction.

None of it is real. All names, places, and events are products of the author's imagination. Any resemblance to real names, places, or events are purely coincidental, and should not be construed as being real.

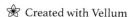

CHAPTER ONE

*C*eleste Blackmoore ducked behind a tall oak tree, her palm resting on the rough ridges of bark as she watched her sister, Jolene, walk down the opposite side of the street. Faded jeans, gray hoodie, long brunette ponytail pulled through the back of her navy-blue Red Sox baseball cap. She looked as if she was on a covert mission, which she probably was, judging by the way she kept glancing behind her as if she was worried someone might be following her.

Celeste slipped out from behind the tree, sending a pile of yellow, orange, and red leaves swirling on the sidewalk as she shuffled through them. She snugged her black leather jacket tighter to ward off the crisp fall air, happy to be out from the shade of the tree and into the sun, where its rays could warm her.

Jolene continued down the street, and Celeste

followed about twenty feet behind. It was noon, but the pedestrian traffic was light, and Celeste had to dart into alcoves and doorways so as not to be spotted. She wasn't really sneaking around behind Jolene's back— she'd happened to see Jolene's car heading out of town and just wanted to catch up with her. Or so she told herself.

So what if she just wanted to hang back a bit and see what had really brought her sister to this small town, a few miles from their hometown of Noquitt, Maine, before announcing her presence? Was that so bad?

If her suspicions about Jolene following up the lead they'd received earlier in the week were true and their adversaries were following the same lead, then Jolene might need her help. Not that Celeste would be much help. She didn't possess the same magically heightened defensive skills as Jolene or her other sisters and was rarely useful in a fight. Come to think of it, her lack of paranormal gifts made her rarely useful on their missions in general.

The four Blackmoore sisters worked for a clandestine government agency that used individuals with paranormal skills on various missions. Most recently, they were tasked with finding twelve ancient energy-infused relics to keep them from falling into the hands of an evil and powerful paranormal, Dr. Bly.

Recently, their contact, Dorian Hall, had passed on

new information on recovering one of the relics—a large energy-infused crystal—rumored to have been hidden somewhere by pirates in the late 1700s. According to her information, a clue to the location had been "hidden in plain sight" in a town in Maine right near them.

The girls had been working all week to narrow down exactly where this clue might be. Jolene was a whiz with the computer, so she was usually the one to do any online research. Knowing Jolene, Celeste figured that she'd found something and come out here to check it out so as to make sure it wasn't a dead end before bringing it to the others. A pang of guilt shot through Celeste. Here she was skulking around behind her sister, almost as if they were in competition or something, but that wasn't the case. The sisters always shared all the clues and worked on their missions together.

But something about their missions had been gnawing at Celeste for quite some time now. The truth was that Celeste felt that she wasn't pulling her weight. She was always in the shadow of her other sisters, who were much more powerful when it came to paranormal abilities.

Her oldest sister, Morgan, was blessed with very strong intuition and a way with herbs. Her sister Fiona had an energy connection with stones and crystals. She could heal mortal wounds and use pebbles as flaming projectiles to fight off enemy paranormals. Jolene was the strongest of them all, being able to sense auras and warp energy in a way that could zap an enemy attacker before they even knew what hit them.

Celeste had none of these gifts. Her only gift being able to talk to ghosts. That hardly ever came in handy when they were being attacked. Sometimes she'd talk to ghosts that would point them in the right direction, but that was just a minor part of their missions. She was afraid she wasn't useful and her sisters only let her tag along because she was related to them.

Even on their last mission to Salem, Massachusetts, where she'd picked up the inklings of the skill of spell casting, she'd felt her efforts had only a minor role in the success of the mission. She hadn't yet successfully honed her skills with charms and spells, but being desperate to prove she could contribute, she'd cast a coaxing spell this morning with the hopes of attracting the clue to her. That was why she was following Jolene. If Jolene had a lead on the clue and Celeste's spell had worked, maybe she could help her sister find it.

Her gaze drifted from Jolene to the shops that lined the street. It was a typical old New England town with brick buildings that dated to the early 1900s. Some had been kept in good condition. Others showed their age with peeling paint and dirty windows.

Dorian had said the clue was hiding in plain sight. Apparently, it had been stored here for decades, quite possibly by George LeBlanc, a treasure hunter from the mid-twentieth century, who had spent his lifetime trying to recover old pirate treasure.

But where would it be hidden?

Celeste scanned the rows of stores. There was a jewelry store, an antique store, a cafe, a sandwich shop, a library... Maybe the clue was hidden in an old book sitting in the library. It wouldn't be the first time the sisters had found a clue in an old book. And a book in the library certainly would be in plain sight.

Her eyes drifted back to Jolene. Jolene wasn't heading toward the library, but Celeste was certain she must be here researching the clue. Why else would she be here? And why would she be glancing around behind her as if she was paranoid?

Jolene turned down a side street, and Celeste picked up the pace, her boot heels making hollow noises on the pavement as she hurried to catch up. She rounded the corner just in time to see Jolene dart into a small alleyway between two tall brick buildings.

Celeste hurried to the opening of the alleyway, slowing just before peeking around the corner. A niggle of trepidation ruffled the hairs on the back of her neck.

Why would Jolene go into an alley?

She glanced at the shops on either side. A Chinese-food restaurant and a gift store. Jolene certainly couldn't be following the clue into the alley here, could she?

Celeste cautiously peered around the corner.

Two hands shot out toward her.

Her heart jerked as someone grabbed her by the sides of her jacket and pulled her into the alley.

Startled, she instinctively moved into one of her karate stances, ready to lash out, fearing that somehow Jolene had wandered into a gathering of paranormal bad guys who were also looking for the clue.

But Jolene was the only one in the alley. And she did not look happy.

"What are you doing following me around?" Jolene demanded even as she let go of Celeste's lapels.

"What are you doing sneaking around?" Celeste straightened her jacket, and the two sisters stared at each other. The alley was shadowed by the buildings on either side, and Celeste felt a chill. Her nose twitched at the smell of pork fried rice and garbage from the rusted blue dumpster at the end of the alley.

Jolene sighed, and her ice-blue eyes—the same color as Celeste's and a Blackmoore family trait—softened. "I'm not sneaking around. I'm hiding from Matteo."

Celeste frowned. She could have sworn Jolene had a thing for Matteo Ortiz, the handsome paranormal who was somewhat of a guardian angel for the sisters.

In fact, during their trip to Salem, Celeste had gotten the distinct impression that the two of them had grown very close. "Why are you hiding from Matteo? I thought you guys were an item."

Jolene scrunched up her face and fiddled with her ponytail. "He's gotten so moony eyed ever since I saved his life. He keeps going on about how we're bonded together forever. It's a turn-off. I don't know if I want to be bonded together with someone. And now he keeps showing up *everywhere*. I liked it better when he was more mysterious and you never knew when he was going to show up."

Celeste's lips quirked up. Wasn't that always the way? Men usually were more appealing when you didn't know if they were interested, especially if they were mysterious and unpredictable like Matteo. Celeste was glad she was over that phase in her life. She'd been seeing her current boyfriend, Cal, for a few years now. They'd been friends since they were kids in a purely platonic way and had recently taken their relationship to a deeper level. Celeste appreciated the stability and comfort of knowing where her relationship was going.

"So, you're not here looking for the clue?" Celeste asked.

Jolene glanced back toward the street. "My research indicated it might be in this town, but I'm not one hundred percent sure. I wanted to scope things out before I wasted everyone's time. And besides, Vinnie's has a great cheese-steak sub, so it was a good excuse to come out and grab one. You want to join me?"

Celeste thought back to earlier in the morning. She'd cast the spell and then headed out to the yoga studio. On the way, she'd seen Jolene's car on Route 1, and her gut instinct had been to follow her. Maybe that hadn't been *just* gut instinct, though. Maybe the spell was working, pulling her toward this town. Toward the clue. "I could go for lunch. But maybe we should do some research first. If the clue were here, where do you think it would be?"

Jolene shrugged. "According to what I discovered, LeBlanc had a shop here in town back in the 1950s."

"He did? That sounds like a good lead. Which shop is it?"

"That's the thing. The shop isn't here anymore. It was somewhat of a novelty shop—a treasure-hunting shop with things for kids and metal detectors and stuff back in the day." Jolene spread her hands. "But it's long gone now."

"But maybe we could find out—"

Crash!

The metal door to the gift store flew open and smashed against the brick side of the building. Two masked men ran out, their dark beards hanging down from hooded masks. They barely glanced at Celeste and Jolene before shoving them out of the way and running out into the street, where a car screeched to a halt. They jumped in, and the car sped off.

"Paranormals!" Jolene yelled and ran after them.

Celeste was about to follow her when she heard moaning from inside the building. Someone was hurt in there. She hesitated for a second. Jolene was a powerful paranormal, but Celeste didn't want to leave her to fight off two guys on her own. Then again, the only defensive skill she had was her karate moves, and that wasn't much protection in a paranormal fight. She was usually more of a hindrance than a help.

"Help me." A weak voice drifted out, and before Celeste knew what she was doing, she'd turned and run inside.

An old man lay on the floor. A gash on his forehead dripped blood down his cheek. He turned when he heard her come in, his eyes sparking with anger then flooding with relief when he realized she wasn't one of the thieves.

She bent down next to him. "What happened? Are you okay?"

"Dang hoodlums." He swatted away her attempts at helping him up. "I can get up. I'm not hurt bad."

He struggled to sit up, and Celeste stepped back, letting him do it on his own. She could see that it was a matter of pride for the old man, and other than the gash on his head, he seemed fine. Still, she readied herself in case he wobbled or fell.

The man pulled himself upright by holding onto the edge of the counter and then brushed the dirt off his tan chinos.

"Thank you, young lady. I think I'm okay." He glanced at the open back door and out into the alley. "I don't suppose you saw which way they went."

Jolene appeared in the doorway, her face concerned. "They took off in a car, but the plate was covered in mud, so I couldn't get it."

Her eyes met Celeste's, and she gave her a knowing look. Obviously, the man would think it was a regular robbery, but the girls knew better. Apparently, Dorian Hall hadn't been the only one to receive the clue.

Jolene pushed the back door shut and tested the lock. "It still works. Did they damage anything in the shop? What did they take?"

The man gestured toward a knocked-over display. "They didn't do much damage, just kicked this over and yelled a lot. You ask me, they had more brawn than smarts."

"Why do you say that?" Jolene picked up the display and started putting the items back on it.

Celeste watched her pick up small treasure chests and fake bags of gold. Looking around, she saw the store was some sort of specialized gift shop, a section of which capitalized on local legends and lore, like the many pirate legends tied to the coast of Maine. Her heartbeat picked up the pace. Pirates were rumored to have hidden the very relic they were looking for.

"They came in here all hepped up, looking for old inventory." The man glanced toward an open door, beyond which Celeste could see stairs leading to the basement. "They made me let them into the basement, and they went down and took some of the old stored boxes. Then they clonked me on the head and took off out into the alley. They didn't even bother with the cash register."

"Can we see what's down there?" Jolene asked.

"Ain't much there, but I guess so." The man started toward the stairs then turned and narrowed his eyes. "You don't think they were looking for drugs or something, do you? I don't have any drugs in here. Seems strange they would leave the money in the cash register."

"I don't think they were looking for drugs. I think they might've been looking for something that had been stored here a long time ago. Has this store been here for a long time?" Jolene asked.

The man continued down the stairs, and they followed, the air becoming moldy as they descended into the dimly lit area. "I've owned the store for a good twenty years. Bought it from an old treasure hunter. Course, he had it set up all different. He was into treasure hunting and had all kinds of treasure paraphernalia. But that's a small market, and people don't do much treasure hunting now, so I added in general gift store items shortly after I bought him out."

The basement was surprisingly empty. A few water-stained cardboard boxes were lined against one wall. Another had wood shelving loaded with seashells, boxes of sunglasses, rubber coin purses, and some old pirate hats.

"Is this all the old storage?" Jolene asked. "Those guys only had two boxes, and there doesn't seem like very much here for an old shop that has been through two owners and around for decades."

"Well, I don't like to keep a lot of old inventory. There's no sense in it. I have a lot of big sales to get rid of the excess," the man said.

Celeste's heart plummeted. "So all the inventory from the original store has been sold off in yard sales?"

"Now, I didn't say that. I said I sell off *my* stuff. Still haven't gotten around to selling off old George's stuff."

"Is that what is in these boxes?" Jolene waved her arm to indicate the cardboard boxes.

"Nope. The original store was much bigger, but over the years, we got less and less traffic, so I moved into this smaller building and rented the original to Slim Lee at the Lucky Dragon." The man nodded toward the alley side of the store. "I never did get around to moving all the old boxes out of the basement, though, so I reckon they're still over there."

CHAPTER TWO

*I*t turned out that the storage boxes *were* still in the basement of the Lucky Dragon. Not only that, but the old man was more than happy to sell the useless inventory to Celeste and Jolene for five hundred dollars.

The girls happily paid him then headed back to their house in Noquitt with five boxes of old inventory to sort through and an oversized paper bag filled with Chinese takeout.

Celeste, Jolene, and their sisters, Morgan and Fiona, lived in their ancestral family home along with their mother, Johanna. The house was a big old three-story mansion with dozens of rooms. It sat on a prime piece of land with the Atlantic Ocean on one side and the channel that led to Perkins Cove on the other. It had been in their family for over three hundred years.

It had stood there long before the fishermen's shacks alongside the water had turned into trendy shops and the cove itself had been dredged to accommodate the dozens of lobstering, fishing, and sailboats that called it home. Generations of Blackmoores had expanded on and added to the house. The quaint town of Perkins Cove had grown to a tourist haven, but the house itself still stood alone on the cliff, overlooking the ocean in the same spot first purchased by their ancestor Isaiah Blackmoore.

But even though they had so many rooms to choose from, the sisters always gravitated to the small sitting room off the kitchen when they wanted to plan and discuss their missions. Maybe it was the soft muted colors or the comfy overstuffed furniture or the large bay window that boasted an unobstructed view of the Atlantic Ocean. Whatever the reason, that was where they sat now with the store boxes laid out on the floor, a pile of square white plates sitting on the desk and the savory smell of eggrolls and sweet-and-sour chicken wafting from the white Chinese-food containers strewn about the coffee table.

"Did you get crab rangoon?" Johanna Blackmoore stood in the doorway that led to the kitchen. Celeste's heart constricted at the sight of her. There had been a time in Celeste's life when she thought she would never see her mother again. The girls had been led to believe she'd jumped into the ocean from the cliffs outside their home, but she'd really been captured by Dr. Bly, whose intent was to drain her of her paranormal energy.

When they had rescued Johanna after over a decade of captivity, she had been a mere shadow of her former self. Her hair had been completely leached of color, and she was barely able to walk, depending on a wheelchair for mobility. Now she looked fit and healthy, her hair a glossy black, with a silver streak down one side as the only reminder of her ordeal.

Celeste picked a few pieces of crab rangoon out of one of the containers, plunked the puffy fried dough pouches on a plate, and handed it to her mother. Johanna showed off by expertly balancing the large triangle of fried dough between two chopsticks and taking a dainty nibble from the corner. "What do you have in the big boxes?"

"I can't say for sure, but it's possible one of these boxes might contain the clue that Dorian told us about," Jolene said.

"You found the clue?" Fiona stood in the doorway. A tangle of long red curls framed her face as her ice-blue eyes drifted from the boxes on the floor to the food containers. "Is that Chinese? I hope you got egg rolls."

"Yes, we got egg rolls. And we're not certain about the clue, but I think there is a good possibility." Celeste told her about their run-in with the paranormals who had stolen the box from the basement of the gift shop and how the real old inventory had been in the basement of the Golden Dragon all along.

"So they took the wrong box?" Fiona asked.

"It would appear so." Jolene flipped open one of the lids and looked inside. "Ha! Looks like old treasure chests in here."

"Treasure chests?" Morgan came into the room, a steaming cup of tea in her hand. She bent over to look in the box, her silky, straight long black hair hanging down over her face like a curtain. "Plastic. Too bad it's not real treasure."

The girls laughed. They didn't really need treasure. They had more than enough money due to an odd discovery in the cliffs below their house, which had likely been hidden by Isaiah Blackmoore, who was rumored to have been a pirate. They didn't even really need to work, but putting their paranormal skills to use for the good of mankind was about more than money.

"Do you think I should call Luke?" Morgan put down the tea and pulled her cell phone out of the back pocket of her jeans. Her boyfriend, Luke, was their contact in the government agency. He usually sourced all the resources they needed for their various missions.

"I can call Jake, too. If we've got a lead, he might be able to do some research," Fiona said.

"Maybe we should make sure this isn't a wild goose chase first." Jolene pushed the box aside and opened another one. Jake Cooper, Fiona's boyfriend, had a private detective agency, and Jolene worked for him. Celeste knew she was still trying to prove herself so that he would trust her to spend more time out in the field and less time behind her desk. Calling him out only to find that the boxes held nothing but old junk probably wouldn't help her cause.

"*Meow!*"

"Looks like Belladonna thinks we should call them." Johanna nodded toward the white cat that had stalked into the room and was busy sniffing the boxes. The cat's gaze snapped up to the Chinese-food containers, her pink nose tilting in the air for a few sniffs before she returned her attention to the boxes from the store. She sniffed each corner then jumped atop one and batted the lid with her paw. She turned serious ice-blue eyes on Celeste. "*Meow.*"

"I think she wants you to take that box, Celeste." Jolene shoved the box toward her sister. "We can each take one. Someone call out if you find anything interesting."

Everyone got busy looking inside their boxes. Just as the man from the store had told them, they were full of treasure-hunting giftware. Not real treasure, the fake treasure that one might buy when on vacation. Souvenirs of the beach, fake pirate coins, books on metal detecting, tiny bottles with letters in them, jars of sand, and even rocks. In Celeste's box, there was an added surprise—old fortune cookies that did not look the least bit appealing.

"Look at these." Celeste pulled a crumbly dark triangle out of the box. "These must be older than the restaurant."

"That's better than what I found. Mine's full of junk," Morgan said.

"Me too." Fiona pushed her box away.

"Ditto. In both boxes here." Jolene sat back and sighed.

"Mine was full of plastic junk, sand, and a weird rock." Celeste pointed to a large piece of chipped rock she'd placed on the coffee table then frowned down at the small strip of yellowed paper in her hand with a three-line fortune. The cookies had been crumbled and broken. Most of the fortunes themselves must have disintegrated. "And these fortunes. On the bright side, this fortune says I'll find great riches, and it looks like I have a lot of lucky letters. This thing is old as the hills. Looks like a funky font. Maybe Cal would be interested in it."

"I'm definitely interested in that." Celeste turned to show him the piece of paper, but his sapphire eyes were fixated on the rock on the table. "Where did you guys get it?"

"It was in these boxes. They came from the old

inventory of a store that we thought might have been related to the clue Dorian got earlier this week," Celeste said.

Cal squatted in front of the coffee table and ran his fingertips lightly over the surface of the rock, which Celeste could now see appeared to have some unnatural indentations. She hadn't noticed it before because the indentations were worn from centuries of weather and the face of the rock was partially covered in lichen.

"Anyway, it doesn't seem like the clue is in here. This is all just junk. Looks like my research was wrong," Jolene said.

"No, I don't think your research was wrong." Cal picked up the rock and turned it toward them. "See these indentations? These are old inscribed letters. And see how the rock is jagged here, almost like it broke off from a bigger piece?"

They all nodded their heads.

"Well, if my guess is correct, it did break off from a bigger rock. A rock on Rune Island."

Jolene's brows shot up, and she held her hand out for the rock. Studying the front, she nodded. "That's right. I remember reading about Rune Island. It's up near Nova Scotia, isn't it?"

"Yes. It's been sort of a mystery for decades, but many swear that pirate treasure is buried there," Cal said.

"Captain Kidd is rumored to have stashed all kinds

of things, but that's not all. They say there might even be treasure from the Knights Templar and even some secret documents that prove Sir Francis Bacon actually wrote the works of Shakespeare." Jolene handed the rock to Fiona. "But that's not the most interesting part. The most interesting thing is that some believe Marie Antoinette's lost jewels were buried there."

"And I heard those lost jewels might contain a powerful stone." Fiona looked up from her study of the rock. "A stone that could turn out to be the relic we're looking for."

Morgan reached for the rock. "I've heard about Rune Island too. I heard it was cursed. Haven't most of the fortune hunters who attempted to find treasure there died mysteriously?"

"Yes, I've even heard of it being called the Island of Fatal Fortunes," Jolene said.

"Sounds like paranormal activity to me," Celeste said.

"All the more reason to check it out." Jolene slipped behind the desk and tapped on her keyboard. "I'm going to see if I can get any details on these jewels. We already know the relic was infused with powerful properties that allow it to absorb and deflect negative energy, kind of like an amped-up version of our amulets."

Celeste's fingers curled around the obsidian amulet

that hung from a leather cord at her throat. Fiona had made one for each of the sisters as protective shields from negative-energy assaults, and they always wore them just in case. They never knew when Bly's guys would jump out from behind a rock or building and try to blast them with negative energy that could render them helpless.

"And it's quite beautiful. They say the moonstone reflects the colors of the rainbow more intensely than any other moonstone in existence," Morgan said.

"And we know it's orb shaped and about twenty-five millimeters long. If there was such a stone in her jewels, then I say we head straight to Rune Island," Jolene added.

"*Mew.*" Belladonna jumped into Morgan's lap and rubbed her cheek on the side of the stone.

"Belladonna seems to agree, and we all know she's never wrong." Morgan handed the stone back to Cal. "But what exactly are the symbols?"

"Rumor has it the symbols were etched hundreds of years ago by pirates as sort of a treasure map to where they buried their loot. Everyone thought that was just a legend until the late 1950s, when someone discovered part of a rock with old etchings. The problem is no one could ever decipher it because part of it was missing." Cal held the rock up. "And now we might have the missing piece."

"So you can figure out exactly where the treasure

is?" Johanna asked. "This should be the easiest mission yet."

"I wish," Cal said. "I still need to decode it. I'm sure I can do it. I'll just need some time to figure out which letter each symbol represents."

"But how did it get in the box?" Johanna asked.

"I bet LeBlanc put it in there. He was one of the last people to look for treasure on the island decades ago. He might've found the rock there, or maybe he got it some other way and had it stored away until the next time he could go to the island." Jolene's fingers flew over the keyboard, her eyes never leaving the screen. "According to my research, he died suddenly of a heart attack. Maybe he planned to go back with the rock and never got the chance."

"Or maybe someone made sure he never got the chance," Fiona said.

"The message Dorian received did say it was hidden in plain sight, right?" Morgan asked.

Johanna nodded and shoved half of a crab rangoon in her mouth. "I have it over here." She went over to the desk and slid open the drawer then pulled out a piece of paper—a copy of an old note that had made its way to Dorian's possession and kicked off the mission in the first place.

X MARKS *the spot*

The key is hidden in plain sight
My fortune is resolved.

"X MARKS THE SPOT," Fiona said. "Sure sounds like it has to do with finding buried treasure to me."

"And the key"—Celeste pointed at the rock—"was hidden in plain sight. Right in this box in the basement. Lucky for us it was in the basement of the wrong building, or those thieves would have gotten it. I'm sure those were Bly's men following the same lead we are."

"Bingo!" Jolene turned the computer to face them. On the screen was a painting of Marie Antoinette wearing a fancy detailed blue silk dress and an elaborate necklace with different-shaped jewels around her neck.

Jolene pointed to the center, where there was a large orb-shaped stone that glittered with rainbow iridescence. "I hope you can figure out that code quickly, Cal, because this necklace is the lost jewels of Marie Antoinette rumored to have been buried on the island, and if I'm not mistaken, that stone in the middle is exactly like the relic we're looking for."

CHAPTER THREE

"Y ou'd think Dorian could have sprung for a helicopter to get us out to the island." Morgan stood on the dock with a large black duffel bag at her feet, her ice-blue eyes scanning the choppy ocean in front of them.

Celeste followed her gaze. Off in the distance, she could barely see the hazy blue mass of land that was Rune Island. "At least they came through with the puddle jumper to get us up here."

"And all the equipment." Fiona pointed toward the street at the end of the dock. Luke, Jake, Cal, and two of the guys who worked for Luke—Gordie and Sam— were unloading various boxes of equipment from the cab that had taken them from the small airport to the marina. The marina itself was small, with only a few boats at the dock. This late in the season, there weren't many who still had boats in the water, and they'd been lucky to find someone who was willing to take them out to the island.

"*Merowww!*" Belladonna screeched inside her soft-sided cat carrier. The cat had been very vocal with her displeasure at being forced to stay in the carrier. She'd wailed the whole trip, and the constant meowing was starting to give Celeste a headache.

Celeste bent down, trying to appease her and, hopefully, shut her up. "Sorry, buddy, but until we get on the island, we want to keep you safe."

"*Meroop!*"

"I don't think you can reason with a cat."

Celeste whirled around upon hearing the voice, to see that a child in a wheelchair had come up behind her. She guessed him to be about eight or nine, with shaggy blond hair and wide blue eyes that shone with the excitement only a child could have, tempered by a tinge of sadness that a child should never have.

"Well, hello there. What's your name?" Celeste asked.

"Christian. Are you treasure hunters?" Christian's curious bright eyes watched Gordy and Luke heft a box of scuba gear onto the lobster boat that would take them to the island. He pushed his fingers in through the mesh of the cat carrier, and Celeste noticed they were thin and twisted. A pang of sorrow ripped through her for the obviously bright and intelligent child who was clearly not in good physical health.

"I guess we are treasure hunters of sorts," she said.

"I thought so. Only treasure hunters or pirates ever go to the island."

"Have you seen pirates out there?" Celeste teased.

Christian smiled and continued to stroke Belladonna with his gnarled fingers. The cat had finally shut up and was actually purring now as she rubbed her head against the boy's fingertips.

"I haven't *seen* any, but I heard they might be there. I don't get to play with the other kids. I mostly sit inside and read pirate books." Christian nodded toward a small weather-beaten cottage near the docks. "That's how I knew you were either a treasure hunter or pirate, as those would be the only people going to the island."

"You live in that cottage?" Celeste asked. It looked barely big enough for two people. Though the tiny yard with its three-foot patch of grass was neatly kept, the white-painted trim needed scraping, and the roof looked about ready to be re-shingled.

Christian nodded, his focus now on petting Belladonna, who was practically asleep. "Me and my dad. My mom's dead."

"Oh, I'm sorry."

"She died when I was a baby." He looked up at her,

his blue eyes curious under his dark lashes. "It must be a real thrill to go on a treasure hunt."

"It *sounds* thrilling, but it can be a lot of hard work."

"Were almost ready to shove off." Jason Hale, the man who would take them to the island in his lobstering boat, came to stand beside her. His weathered face made him look much older than his age, which Celeste guessed to be midthirties. She also guessed that it was more than hard work on the open seas that had aged him. He ruffled Christian's hair affectionately. "Why don't you head on home, buddy? Layla will stay with you. I'll only be gone a couple hours while I take them out."

Christian's face fell. He glanced at the island then back at his father, pasting a resigned smile on his face as if he was accustomed to disappointment. "Okay, Dad."

Celeste watched him wheel his way back to the house.

"He's a good boy," Jason said.

"He seems smart."

"Too smart for his own good sometimes. Too bad his mind is so sharp, but his body is failing him," Jason said.

"What's wrong with him?"

"Rare autoimmune disease. The doctors up here can't help him. There's some alternative treatments, but those take a lot of money, and meanwhile, he's fading away." His voice hitched, and then he took a deep breath. "Well, you didn't come here to listen to my troubles. Let's get you on the boat and over to the island."

Having grown up on Perkins Cove, Celeste had been on dozens of lobster boats. Jason's boat was a large one, painted a practical gray and white. Celeste noted with approval that it was kept in good condition and clean as a whistle, though it did smell faintly of fish. Fishy smells never came out, no matter how much cleaning you did. Christian must have worked some magic on Belladonna, and she slept peacefully in her carrier as they loaded the rest of the equipment onto the back platform, where Jason had removed the towers of metal lobster traps.

Jason started the motor, and Cal and Luke cast off the thick ropes then jumped on board as Jason pulled away from the dock. Celeste made her way along the narrow walkway to the bow, her heart heavy as she glanced back toward the house to see Christian waving enthusiastically as they headed out.

Celeste wondered about the alternative treatments for the boy. Could he possibly be cured or at least have his quality of life improved? She wanted to ask Jason what his chances were, but it was none of her business, and even though Jason had volunteered information on Christian's conditions on his own, she had learned long ago that people didn't like it when others dug too deeply into their business.

It was clear Jason didn't have any money to pay for the treatments, but Celeste and her sisters had more money than they could ever use. That money was all tied up in trusts and retirement funds and guarded zealously by teams of lawyers. It would take an act of Congress to free any of it up to give to Jason for Christian's treatment. And Celeste had the feeling Jason would be too proud to take the money. She sighed and turned to face the front, looking toward the island. Rumor had it that pirate treasure was buried there. If she found some, could she somehow get it to Jason for Christian's treatment?

Even though they weren't going to Rune Island to look for pirate treasure other than the necklace, it was likely they might find some. The sisters were only interested in getting the relic. None of them cared about any monetary gain that might come from additional treasure. So, if she happened to find a few gold pirate coins lying around, maybe she could slip them to Jason on the return trip.

If she couldn't help her sisters on their missions or fight paranormals, maybe she could at least help *someone*. The thought of it brightened her outlook and made her eager to get to the island.

"I know what you're thinking." Cal slipped his arm around her shoulders, and she snuggled into his warmth. Now that they were out to sea, it had turned colder, and the wind bit through her down jacket. She pulled the brown-striped wool cap that she'd stuffed over her short-cropped blond hair down further to cover the tips of her ears. Thankfully, they'd known the fall temperatures would be cool on the island and had dressed accordingly.

"What am I thinking?" She leaned back and looked up into Cal's eyes. What she saw in the depths still caused a flutter in her stomach, even though they'd known each other practically their whole lives.

"You're thinking about that little boy and how you can help him."

Celeste smiled and shrugged. "Maybe."

Was she that transparent? Or was it just that Cal knew her so well? Either way, it felt good to have someone like Cal on her side. "Maybe we can find a way. But first we need to recover the relic. Have you made any headway on decrypting the symbols on the rock?"

"Unfortunately, no. It's a very sophisticated cipher. I've tried all the basics for decoding it, and no dice. This one is going to take some work."

"We may not need to decode it," Luke said. He and Morgan had joined them at the bow. Morgan's long black hair whipped around her face. "We already know several spots on the island that are reputed to have treasure. My team has done some thorough research, and we have a few starting points we can tackle while you work on decrypting. There's even a big hole that people have dubbed the Treasure Pit that leads to a maze of caves where it seems likely the treasure would have been stashed."

Jolene had been listening from her spot next to the pot hauler. "I'm worried more about *who* we might find out there."

"From what I can gather, it's been abandoned for decades. It used to be a hotspot for treasure hunters, but literally no one goes there anymore. Too many unexplained deaths," Luke said.

"Probably at the hands of Dr. Bly or his predecessors," Jolene said. "But now that this new clue has surfaced, I bet we might see a resurgence in popularity for the island."

Cal pressed his lips together. "Whoever stole the boxes from the gift store think they have the clue. But they won't know it points to Rune Island. We didn't know until I recognized the writing on that rock, and besides, the boxes they stole wouldn't have had that rock in them."

"So they could be looking in a totally different direction," Morgan said.

"For now. But they are bound to figure it out sooner or later," Jolene pointed out. "I'm sure Bly has people watching us, and once he gets word we're here, he's sure to send people to follow."

"If he hasn't already," Celeste said.

"I bet Jason could tell us if there has been activity on the island." Luke headed back toward the wheelhouse, and they all followed.

The wheelhouse was just a covered shelter that was open in the back and had windows on the side. Jason stood in front of an oak ship's wheel, various gadgets and electronics on the dashboard in front of him. He hadn't asked many questions and was happy to charge the fee that Dorian had paid. Celeste knew why. The man needed money. And if he did, maybe he'd taken someone else out here too.

"Do you take many people out to the island?" Luke asked.

Jason's eyes narrowed. "Rune Island? No one wants to go there. I don't think I've taken anyone out in ages. Young folks sometimes, maybe a tourist or two, but usually just for the day, and only in summer. It's colder on that island than the mainland. Plus it's pretty well known the island is haunted after the mysterious deaths years ago. People seem to steer clear."

"So, it's totally abandoned?" Jolene asked.

"Yep. There's not much out there to see. Just some old cabins and holes in the ground. It's isolated. No plumbing or electricity. The coastline is all rocks, so there's not even a nice beach." Jason studied them.

"We we're just wondering if we might expect to run into other people," Morgan said.

"I think you'll be all alone out there. You need privacy for your documentary?"

Dorian had used her US government persuasion to get permission to use the island. It was unclear to Celeste and her sisters who owned it, but they didn't really need to know that. As long as they had permission and were there on behalf of the government, they were good to go.

"We don't like to be surprised is all," Jolene said. "Need to figure out where to shoot and can't have random people showing up."

"I'm pretty sure you guys will be the only ones out there," Jason said.

"But you wouldn't be the only person to bring people out here," Cal said. "Someone could have gotten there on a another boat, right?"

"Doubtful. As you can see, not too many boats are in the water up here this time of year. And my marina is the only one for miles. Besides, the place is haunted and booby-trapped, and if there ever was any treasure on it, I'm sure it was found long ago." Jason's gaze drifted over the gray sea to the fast-approaching island. "Nope. I'm sure you people are the only ones crazy enough to go out there this time of year."

CHAPTER FOUR

*T*he Rune Island dock was nothing fancy. About twenty feet of weathered boards were built over the jetty of rocks that seemed to make up the entire perimeter of the island. Jason helped them stack the gear on the dock then gave them his cell number with instructions to call when they wanted to be picked up, before casting off and leaving them alone on the island. Or at least they hoped they were alone.

Celeste hefted her backpack on one shoulder and her sleeping bag on the other and followed the others up the sloping hill that Jason had said led to the cabins. Here on the unprotected jetty, she could feel the sting of cold salt air on her cheeks and noticed her sisters tightening their hoods and tucking their chins into their jackets. Though it was only mid-fall, it was much colder on an island in the middle of the Atlantic than it had been on the mainland.

"Jason said the cabins are in a more protected area. We shouldn't have to deal with this wind there." Cal walked backwards as he talked, loaded down with camping gear and wrestling one of the big coolers on wheels over the rocky terrain.

"Good thing. I just hope they are habitable," Fiona said.

"Umm, barely."

They'd come to the top of a hill. Below, five cabins sat in a semicircle. They were old wooden structures shingled with cedar shakes that had weathered to a dull gray. Some had the windows still intact, but others sported boards where some of the windows should be.

"They don't look so bad. At least they're solid." Luke started toward the cabins, and they all followed. As Jason had said, the cabins were situated in a valley that protected them from the wind, which died down as they got closer.

To say the cabins had a rustic charm would have been stretching things, but from their wide front porches, to the homemade shutters, to the window boxes—now just full of dirt and dead plants—they weren't completely unappealing.

"It's not quite like the hotels we're used to." Fiona climbed up on the porch of the first one and pushed open the door. Inside, it was surprisingly clean, with a solid wood floor, a small kitchenette in one corner, and a cast-iron wood stove in the main room. A doorway led to another room in the back—the bedroom, Celeste assumed.

Though the sisters had been lucky enough to stay in nice hotels on most of their missions, Celeste didn't think this was *too* bad. At least they'd be warm and dry, and hopefully, it would only be for a few nights anyway.

"You're spoiled." Jake slid his arm around Fiona's shoulders. "Don't worry. This will be fun. Like camping."

"It's a bit chilly for camping." Morgan snugged her purple down vest tighter around her middle.

"Don't worry. We can zip our bags together." Luke winked at her.

"It is what you make of it. I have dibs on this little cabin on the end." Jolene's voice was cheery, though she looked a little sad as she started toward the end cabin. She was the only one without a significant other. Was she missing Matteo? He usually didn't accompany them on their missions, but somehow, he always showed up to help out. Maybe not this time, though. Things hadn't been the same after what had happened between him and Jolene in Salem.

"We'll take this one if no one else minds." Fiona pointed to the one whose porch she was standing on.

"It's all the same to me. How about we take the next one?" Celeste glanced at Cal.

"Sounds good."

"Okay, that leaves this other one for us since Buzz and Gordy have tents. We'll get unpacked and situated." Luke put the bags he was carrying down. "Gordy, you and Buzz go scope out the island and see if you can find evidence of anyone else here."

Buzz and Gordy headed off, and the rest of them set to work unpacking Coleman lanterns, cookstoves, sleeping bags, an outdoor shower, and plenty of propane in medium-sized cylinders.

There was a big fire pit in the center of the cabins, and Cal got a fire going. Before long, it looked more as if they were on a leisurely fall retreat than on a potentially dangerous hunt for an old relic.

Jake popped open the lid of one of the big coolers. "Steaks?"

"Yes!" several of them answered at the same time.

He pulled out a bunch of rib eyes and some potatoes, which the girls wrapped in tinfoil then shoved into the red-hot center of the fire. Morgan produced a red-and-white-checked tablecloth and covered the top of the two picnic tables then set condiments and napkins on top of that.

She stood back to survey her work. "All the comforts of home."

Luke and Jake tended to the steaks, which sizzled

on top of fire grates. Fiona and Jolene found some paper plates, cups, a gallon of water, and a six-pack of beer. Celeste made a salad. Soon, they were sitting at the table with a feast laid out in front of them.

Gordy came back just as they were starting to eat, and they shifted positions to accommodate him at the table.

"There's no one else on the island right now." Gordy picked up a potato, shuffling the hot package from one beefy hand to the other as he tried to free it from the tinfoil. He placed it on his plate and split it open with a knife, the steam swirling up into the air. "The island is shaped like a cone, with a high point at the north end. It's a great vantage point. Buzz stayed up there to keep watch while I picked up some grub. I'll bring him supper, and then he and I will take turns keeping watch from up there."

"Excellent work." Luke passed him the butter. "Did you see anything else of interest?"

Gordy shrugged. "Not really. There's a cove on the south side that looks dredged out. Unnatural. I figure that might have some caves like you said."

"Maybe that's where the intake caverns are that flood the tunnels," Cal said.

"Or where pirates hid treasure," Jolene suggested.

"We need to check it all out," Luke said. "Let's discuss our plan of attack."

"Have you figured anything else out about the inscriptions, Cal?" Morgan asked.

Cal pressed his lips together. He'd already finished eating and had a photo of the inscribed rock in front of him, a pencil and paper in his hand. "I'm afraid not. The rock from the basement is only half the story."

Luke frowned. "What do you mean?"

"See this?" Cal held up a picture of another rock similar to the one they'd found. "This is the rock that was found years ago. It's in the Orthon Treasure Museum now, but it's clearly from the same rock as the one we found in the box." He pushed the pictures of the two rocks together. "You can see that the one we found broke off from this larger rock."

"Yep."

"But look." Cal pointed to the other edge of the rock. "It appears there is supposed to be more. There aren't enough letters on these two rocks to give much direction. Something is missing, but I can still decipher what I have. That might help us figure out some of the steps leading to the treasure."

"That would narrow things down, right?" Luke asked.

"Hopefully." Cal didn't look up from his notebook.

"So we need to scour the island for another rock?" Jake asked.

"Hopefully, that rock is still *on* the island and we can find it," Luke said.

Cal made a sweeping gesture with his right arm. "Even if it is, it would be like looking for a needle in a haystack."

"Still, I'll have Gordy and Buzz look while they are on watch," Luke said.

"That would help." Cal returned his attention to his work. "As you can see, there aren't nearly enough letters here for it to give much instruction as to where the treasure is, but it could get us close... *if* I can break the code."

"*Mew.*" Belladonna had been trotting from person to person, shooting pointed looks at their forks as they ferried the steak from their plates to their mouths. Apparently, it was Celeste's turn. The cat had jumped up on the bench beside her, tilting her head to the left, her ice-blue eyes flicking from Celeste's face to her plate.

"Fine. Here." Celeste cut off a tiny piece, and Belladonna took it and ran under the table.

"I fed her earlier." Jolene peeked under the table. "You're going to get fat if you overeat."

"*Merow!*"

"So what do we do in the meantime?" Morgan asked.

"We have plenty of places to start looking even without the treasure map, and we have to start somewhere until Cal can get more information out of that rock." Luke started clearing away the plates, taking them to a big tub where Morgan had soapy water ready for cleaning.

"What about the treasure pit?" Jake said. "Dozens of treasure hunters before us can't have been wrong about that being a likely place to find treasure."

"Isn't that where all the deadly accidents have happened?" Fiona asked.

"Yes, but we're smarter than those regular treasure hunters, and we have a secret weapon." Luke pointed to the four sisters, implying their paranormal gifts could help protect them against accidents similar to those that had befallen the others who had come to the island.

"True," Morgan said. "Those other accidents were probably paranormal in origin. Dr. Bly or his predecessors might have been here to cause them. Normal people would be no match for their unusual powers, but we'll be well armed to take care of them."

"I don't like the idea of you girls going in there," Luke said. "Even though we know no one else is on the island, the tunnels could be unstable after all these years. It could be dangerous."

Morgan glared from her spot crouched in front of the tub. "We've been in dangerous tunnels and caves before. You know we can take care of ourselves."

"I know, but—"

"It's the best plan to have us go in," Jolene cut in. "We have the abilities to sense if there is a paranormal presence. Fiona can get a read on the different rocks inside the caves, I can look for negative energy, and Morgan can amp up her intuition to tell us if someone has laid a trap recently. We'll be fine. And, besides, we need to divide and conquer. Some of us should go into the treasure pit, but some of us should check out some of the other potential areas on the island. There's no guarantee the relic is in the treasure pit."

"That's right." Fiona grabbed a dish towel to dry the dishes Morgan was washing. "It will take us too long if we explore every area together."

"You have a point," Luke said. "But I want you girls to go in together."

"I can go too. By morning, I'll need a break to let my subconscious work on this code," Cal said.

Luke nodded. "Okay, then. You stay up top near the mouth of the cave. From what I've seen, we might need to climb down in, so let's use a rope lead line, and you can tug on it to alert Cal if you run into trouble."

"Okay."

"We'll stay in contact through the satellite walkie-talkies. They probably won't work in the caves, so I'll stay in contact with Cal. Jake and I will take the scuba gear and explore the cove," Luke said.

"Perfect." Morgan stood and stretched her back, looking out over the ocean toward the west, where a bright-pink sun kissed the top of the sea, painting the bottoms of the clouds with splashes of purple and pink. "Red sky at night, sailor's delight."

"Yeah, I heard it was going to be nice tomorrow," Cal said. "Indian summer. Should be in the seventies."

"That's good. I don't love the idea of getting into the Atlantic Ocean this time of year, but at least it won't be freezing," Jake said.

"We should pack it in early and start first thing. We'll need to be well rested and on our toes..." Jolene rambled on about how they would use their best practices to make sure they were safe. How she would keep an eye out for negative energy. How Morgan could amp up her intuition to sense if someone was after them. How Fiona could try to use her skills with rocks to figure out the likely treasure-hiding places and maybe even ferret out the stone. If it had been infused with special energy long ago, she might be able to sense where it was.

She didn't mention how Celeste could help, but why should she? Celeste didn't have any special skills that would help them should they get attacked in the tunnels. Unless she could disarm a paranormal with a karate kick, she was pretty much useless.

The only thing she could do was talk to ghosts and cast spells, and even that wasn't working very well. While Cal was engrossed in his decryption and everyone else was talking about the plans for the next day, Celeste slipped away. She'd been drawn toward a cliff that she could see past the last cabin, and she walked slowly in that direction.

It faced east toward the open ocean, and the view was magnificent. Someone had put a thick log lengthwise on its side there long ago, and Celeste sat on it, listening to the pound of the surf on the rocks below. A seagull swooped overhead, its lonely call echoing into the slowly darkening sky. Up above, a crescent moon shone brightly even though the sky was still blue.

She closed her eyes and focused on her breath. Meditating always made her feel better, and soon she felt content. Peaceful.

She was happy to be here with her sisters, and even if she didn't contribute as much as them, she would try to be as helpful as possible. Who knew—maybe one of her spells really would come in handy.

"Why so glum?"

Celeste's eyes snapped open to see a swirling mist of a figure in wide, flowing pants, a flowing sash at its waist, and brandishing what looked like a big, shiny saber.

* * *

THE APPEARANCE of a misty figure was nothing new to Celeste. She was used to talking to ghosts. But this one certainly had the fanciest outfit she'd ever encountered. With the wide-legged pants, scarves, and scabbard, she guessed her to be a pirate.

"Who are you?"

"Mirabella de Lafleur at your service." The ghost bowed, gesturing in front of her in an exaggerated manner, then her face turned serious as she studied Celeste. "Why aren't you with the others? I sense sadness about you."

"I'm not really sad—it's just that my sisters have special gifts, and I don't." That made her sound like a spoiled brat. She was happy that her sisters had these great gifts. "I mean I just wish I could help them more."

Mirabella fisted her hands on her hips. "Oh, I know just how you feel."

"You do?"

"Yep. I bet you contribute more than you think. But your sisters' skills are showier. They get all the credit."

"Well, I wouldn't exactly put it that way."

"Right, but you don't get your fair share. Same exact thing happens to me, matey." Mirabella gestured to her person. "I mean, let's face it—women pirates hardly get any of the credit. It's always about the men. Blackbeard this and Captain Kidd that. I can tell you plenty of women pirates did lots of things that these guys took the credit for."

"No doubt. But my sisters would never take credit for anything I did. It's just that..." Celeste chewed her bottom lip, feeling even more like a jerk. She should be proud of her sisters, not sitting here feeling sorry for herself. "Anyway, that doesn't matter. We're a team, and it doesn't matter who gets credit for what."

"Now, that's the spirit. Besides, I bet you contribute a lot and have lots of special gifts. You're talking to me, and that seems like a pretty good gift. Communicating across three centuries isn't something everyone can do."

Celeste smiled. "Yeah, I guess. So, who are you exactly, and why are you here now?"

Mirabella plopped down next to Celeste on the log and leaned her forearms on her knees. "I used to sail the Caribbean as a privateer and provided my services to those who could afford it. I worked for kings and queens. I've recovered treasure and sent men to watery graves."

"Sounds like you've been busy."

She nodded, her eyes narrowing. "But my last commission was by far my most important."

"Oh?"

"I was commissioned by Marie Antoinette herself on the most important day of the French Revolution to deliver a certain item. I vowed to protect it with my life."

Celeste's pulse quickened. "Her jewels."

Mirabella nodded. "We set sail for the new world. I had a contact there." She looked out over the ocean, her expression turning grim. "But the pirate Jon Dubonnet followed me."

"And you ended up here."

"We saw the sails of the ship behind us and veered off course to lose him. We landed here, and I barely had time to hide my cargo before Dubonnet was upon us." She turned back to Celeste. "He killed us all. And so I've spent that last two hundred and thirty years waiting for you."

"For me?"

"You're the only one so far who has been able to see me. I need you to complete my mission. To get the stone into the right hands. I must honor my vow to protect them, before I can move on."

Celeste nodded. Mirabella was stuck on the physical plane, bound by her vow until the stones were in their rightful place. She would be destined to walk this island as a ghost until then. Celeste felt a surge of compassion for Mirabella and a renewed enthusiasm for their mission.

"Sounds like our goals are aligned," Celeste said. "But you hid the jewel—the relic—long ago, and lots of people have been here since. Is it still here?"

"Arghh. Of that I am sure." Mirabella jumped to her feet and paced in front of Celeste. "Much treasure has been buried here by me and those that came after me, but the jewels... I know no one has yet found them, though it is not for lack of trying. In that sense, Dubonnet has unwittingly helped us."

"Oh, he's still here too?"

Mirabella nodded. "'Fraid so. And attempting to thwart the efforts of every treasure hunter that has come upon the island."

Was Dubonnet's ghost behind all the accidents that had happened on the island? Did Mirabella have anything to do with them?

"Do you know anything about the mysterious deaths that have occurred here?" Celeste asked.

Mirabella looked at her sharply. "Some of it is the doing of Dubonnet. But some of it is the doing of more physical beings. Beings with strange powers."

Paranormals. "And what about you? Were you responsible for any of the accidents?"

"No. I would not harm an innocent treasure hunter." Mirabella's face clouded. "Though I saw many harmed... Perhaps I should have interceded."

"Why didn't you?"

Mirabella looked down at the ground. "I dare not leave this general vicinity."

"Why?"

"My husband and ship navigator, Constantine, was murdered by Dubonnet. I buried him here." Mirabella pointed to a patch of ground that was slightly sunken in, then her gaze drifted out over the ocean. The sky was darkening now, indigo blue in front of them fading to royal blue on the sides. "I wanted him to have a view of the constellations and our beloved sea. I fought on the island for two more days before Dubonnet killed me as well. My body was thrown off the cliff, but I cannot leave Constantine's side now for fear we will not be together in eternity."

"So you don't venture far from this piece of land, then?" Celeste's hopes dimmed. If Mirabella wouldn't leave this cliff, she couldn't show her where the relic was hidden. "I need you to show me where the relic is."

"Nay, I couldn't show you even if I could leave. You see, I gave the relic to Constantine to hide. He etched a treasure map in the rocks while I was fighting Dubonnet's men in case he perished before he could tell me where he'd hidden it. He managed to tell me at least that much, but he was killed before he could show me where it was."

Mirabella must have been referring to the rock they'd found. There was no way two people would have inscribed clues on rocks. "We found part of the rock he etched. It had broken from the main rock, and we need the rest of it. Where is it?"

"I was never able to make it there. I'm not sure about the rock, but Constantine did say something about three large Scotch pines."

Three large Scotch pines? Celeste knew they could grow sixty feet tall, but she hadn't seen any that tall on the island. Then again, they were talking about trees that had been there two hundred years ago. Maybe they no longer existed.

Celeste took another glance around. "Where are those?"

Mirabella waved toward the northwest. "Over there. Can't you see them?"

"No. Didn't he tell you *where* he hid the actual relic?"

"Of course. Well, not exactly, since we had little time, but I can tell you it is buried down below, in the tunnels. There's a natural vein of white quartz sediment in the rocks. A white line that runs along the wall. Follow that to the junction of three tunnels, and take the right-most path. You will see that the line shoots straight up. Go below the line, and you will find the gem."

Hope flickered in Celeste's chest. Maybe she wasn't such a boat anchor after all. The others were back at the camp with no clue as to where to look, and now she had a key piece of information on what to look for.

Celeste pushed up from the log. "Thanks. I promise you I will find the gem and get it to where it was meant to be." She glanced down at the depression in the ground. "Then you and Constantine can be reunited on the other side."

"I'm grateful." Mirabella swirled, drops of mist peppered the ground, then she stopped and came close enough for Celeste to feel her chill. "But you must be careful. Dubonnet's ghost still lurks in the caves, trying to do harm to those who seek the treasure."

It wouldn't be the first time Celeste and her sisters had had to do battle with an angry ghost. Luckily, they had that down to a science, and it was something even Celeste could help with. "Don't worry—we ain't afraid of no ghost."

Celeste turned back toward the cabins, a spring in her step. She felt a kinship with Mirabella, who had always played second fiddle to the male pirates just as Celeste sometimes felt she played second fiddle to her sisters. Her mission would help Mirabella, and now she knew exactly where to look for the relic. Maybe she really was more helpful to their missions than she'd thought.

CHAPTER FIVE

*T*he next day, Celeste was up in time to see the glorious sunrise over the ocean. As promised, it was warmer, allowing for hooded sweat-shirts to be warm enough for the morning. Come noontime, she figured short sleeves would suffice.

The night before, she'd told the others about her conversation with Mirabella, and they'd decided to stick to their original plan, with the girls exploring the cave and the guys going to the cove.

Since Mirabella hadn't been able to tell her exactly where the treasure was buried, they still didn't have an exact destination, although at least now she had some-thing to look for.

The treasure pit had been discovered in the late 1800s, when enterprising treasure hunters noticed the ground was unnaturally sunken in on one area of the island.

They reasoned that pirates had buried treasure hundreds of years earlier in that area, and over the centuries, the ground had sunken in because of the disturbance.

Digging had revealed a series of caves and tunnels. Were they natural or previously dug by pirates to be used as hiding places for treasure?

Armed with mountain-climbing gear and determination, the girls headed toward the area. A large hole had been dug in the center of a depression. Inside the hole was a precarious system of natural steps and rocks that led to a wide opening that was the beginning of the caves. One misstep would send them plunging down hundreds of feet to dark waters below. How deep that water was, no one knew. Celeste didn't care to find out. She double-checked the rope at her waist and followed her sisters down the slippery slope to the mouth of the cave. After one last glance up at the blue sky and Cal's smiling face, she gave him a thumbs-up and disappeared into the gloom.

The mouth of the tunnel was wide, about fifteen feet across and six feet tall. The girls stood in a cluster in the waning patch of light and tied their ropes off to a ring that Morgan had jammed into a crack in the rock. They'd need those ropes to get out.

"*Meow.*" Belladonna trotted into the mouth of the tunnel behind them.

"Where did she come from?" The beam of Fiona's

LED flashlight illuminated Belladonna's white fur. She sat on her haunches as if waiting for further instructions.

"I guess she followed us." Jolene bent and scratched the cat behind the ears. "She'll be okay, right?"

Celeste flipped on her headlamp and shrugged. "She usually is. Besides, I doubt she would leave if we asked her."

"Okay then, which way do we go?" Morgan swooped the beam of her flashlight along the sides of the tunnel, revealing walls of jagged, moist rock. Celeste did the same, looking for the vein of white quartz.

"Hold on," Jolene said. "Let's take a reading and make sure we're not walking into a paranormal trap or something."

She took a deep breath and closed her eyes. Celeste knew that she was amping up her paranormal energy, something her sisters usually kept running at low levels so as not to be overwhelmed with their extrasensory perceptions.

Jolene turned slowly, her gaze sweeping over the ceiling, walls, and floors of the tunnel. Then she stopped. "I don't sense any bad energy. Just a faint yellow-energy trail, but it's kind of hopeful. Nonthreatening. Might be from a bird or animal. Whatever it is is long gone. I don't think there is any danger lurking here."

Morgan nodded. "I agree. My intuition is flat on normal. I think I might be getting a reading from Mirabella or the last people to treasure-hunt here, though, as I sense someone looking for something."

"I don't see anything strange with any of the rocks." Fiona bent down and scooped up a handful of pebbles and put them in her pocket. "It wouldn't hurt for me to be armed with some just in case."

Fiona's special gift was to be able to infuse the energy of rocks. She could take healing carnelian stones and make them ten times more powerful. Celeste had seen her use them to heal an open wound in hours. She'd perfected her gifts so that she could employ regular, everyday rocks and pebbles as defensive weapons. She could infuse them with a red-hot energy and then fling them as projectiles toward their enemies.

"Good. Then we continue on. And there's only one way to go." Jolene pointed toward the dark bowels of the cave. "That way."

The sisters hesitated for a second. Belladonna not so much. She gave a short "mew" then trotted off into the darkness, her white fur looking ghostly against the stark blackness of the tunnel.

"You heard her. Let's go." Morgan aimed her flashlight and moved forward.

The farther into the tunnel they got, the damper the air became. Celeste put the hood of her gray sweatshirt up over her head and tugged the strings together. She used the small penlight in her right hand to periodically sweep the sides of the tunnel, looking for that white vein of quartz, while the brighter light on her head illuminated the path before them.

They walked in silence, the drip, drip, drip, of water somewhere inside the cave and the dull scrape of their hiking boots the only sounds.

"It sure is quiet in here," Jolene whispered. "How many pirates do you think traveled this same path?"

"I hope at least Mirabella's husband was one of them," Fiona said. "I don't see this quartz line you told us about, Celeste."

"He wouldn't have come this way, I don't think. This treasure pit was dug out in the 1800s. A hundred years after Mirabella's time. So they probably entered the cave system at another point, but hopefully, this entry leads to that point," Morgan said.

How many tunnels were in here? What were the odds of them stumbling across the spot Constantine had buried the relic?

"I'll see if I can scare her up tonight and find out more about where the entry point was," Celeste said.

"It's a good thing we have Luke and Jake checking things out from the cove. That might be a more likely place for them to have gained entry," Fiona said.

"A lot has probably changed since Mirabella's time, but these tunnels existed before the men dug in the 1800s," Morgan pointed out. "That's why they dug the treasure pit, because of the indentation. So Constantine could have followed this same path."

"Someone did." Jolene flashed her light on an old metal axe.

"Yeah, someone has been in here for sure." Fiona picked up a rusted buckle off the ground. It was wide, with the buckle side elongated, and had remnants of fancy carving. Definitely not of modern design. "Looks like a shoe buckle, probably from the 1700s."

"So we're on the right path." Jolene shone her light ahead to show a cross section where the tunnel split, with one side going to the right and the other to the left. "Now which way do we go?"

"*Meow!*" Belladonna's cry came from the path on the left.

Celeste swung toward it, her headlamp illuminating something long and white. Beyond it, the path continued but took a sharp dip downward, as if it were going downhill. The cat batted at the white thing, and it spun, clattering hollowly.

"What the heck?" Jolene bent down to look at it. "Holy smokes, it's a bone!"

"Look. Here's more." Fiona moved farther downhill and pointed to a pile of rotting fabric. Amidst the colorful swatches lay a femur, a jawbone, and part of a skeletal hand.

"*Meow!*" Belladonna's voice was insistent as she started back toward the entrance.

"It's okay, Belladonna. He can't hurt us now." Morgan turned back to the skeleton. "Looks like those rumors of accidents weren't just stories."

"*Mew!*" Belladonna looked serious.

"We get the picture. Danger," Jolene said.

"This looks like pirate clothing. I don't think this guy was from the 1950s or even the 1900s," Morgan said.

"But how did he get here, and what happened to him?" Celeste asked.

Jolene frowned. "Do you think your evil pirate had something to do with it?"

"Maybe."

Morgan glanced behind them. "And do you think his ghost could be here waiting to do the same thing to us?"

Celeste shrugged. "He might be here, but he's a ghost and can't really move physical objects, so as long as we don't get caught in his ectoplasmic orbit, we should be fine."

"Umm... maybe." Fiona shone her light on the walls of the tunnel, and they turned toward her.

"What do you mean?" Morgan asked.

"In some cases, ghosts can gain extra energy from

certain rocks that can allow them to manifest in the physical plane," Fiona said. "We're basically surrounded by rock in here, so it's possible Dubonnet could harm us with more than just enveloping us in his ectoplasmic orbit."

"And possible he harmed the treasure hunters that died on the island before us, then," Jolene said.

Fiona nodded and moved a piece of fabric with the toe of her boot and then pulled back quickly. "Look at this."

Beside the fabric was a nasty rusted steel trap, its jagged teeth clamped over the skeleton's ankle.

"Is that one of the booby traps?" Jolene asked.

"Probably," Morgan said. "I heard there were all kinds of traps here, not the least of which were ones that triggered the tunnels to be filled with water. I never heard of a skeleton found still in the trap, though."

"I'm sure the other treasure hunters must have come this way." Jolene yawned. "We should continue down this section."

"*Meowl!*" Belladonna trotted in front of Jolene as if to cut her off.

"What? It's fine. We'll keep our senses amped up, and we have our amulets."

Celeste's chest tightened, and her fingers curled around her amulet.

"*Merooo.*" The cat's insistent yowling was making

Celeste tired. Now Belladonna crouched by the side of the path, batting at something else. Jolene stood over her, making a face.

"What is that?"

"Looks like more bones," Morgan said. "Too small to be human."

"*Meree!*" Belladonna pushed the pile of bones in front of them and started back toward the entrance.

The girls stood in a circle, looking down at them. Fiona stifled a yawn then sat down, picking a few tiny bones up. She squinted up at them. "Some kind of small bird."

"A pirate's parrot?" Morgan slumped down beside Fiona. "This is exhausting."

"Too small to be a parrot." Jolene leaned against the wall, slowly sliding toward a sitting position. "Maybe a parakeet."

"Or a canary." Celeste could barely get the words out. Her head was starting to feel fuzzy, and she joined her sisters on the ground, her head lolling forward.

She was so sleepy.

She slumped over. Her eyes drifted shut as her conscious awareness faded. The last thing she remembered was hearing Belladonna's panicked meows in the distance.

* * *

CAL PEERED ANXIOUSLY into the dark hole of the treasure pit.

Were the girls having any luck in there?

He glanced at his watch. They should be coming out at any time. The agreement was one half hour of exploration.

He peeked in again.

Meow!

A white blur exploded out of the mouth of the tunnel, scampered up the cliff-like steps, and ran straight to him.

"Belladonna? What is it?"

The cat was acting crazy, pacing in front of him and then running back to the cliff. That could only mean one thing. The girls were in trouble!

Cal didn't have any ropes or other gear, but he tore down the narrow cliff steps without hesitation and dove into the mouth of the cave. Once inside, he blundered into the darkness, fumbling in his pocket for the small flashlight he'd stuffed in there earlier in the day.

His heart hammered in his chest as he switched it on, illuminating the tunnel. There was no sign of Celeste or her sisters. Up ahead, Belladonna cried out, and he rushed forward, following the sound of her frantic meows.

"Celeste! Jolene!" His yells echoed through the tunnel, but there was no answer, just the cries of the panicked cat.

He rushed on, thankful there was only one direction in which to go. The sound of the meows grew louder until he came to the split-off. Swiveling toward the sound of Belladonna's voice, he illuminated four heaps on the ground.

"Celeste!"

He rushed toward her, but Belladonna leapt in front of him as if trying to stop him. Clearly, she wanted him to find the girls, but it also seemed as if she was trying to keep him from going toward them.

Was there something wrong in there? Maybe one of Bly's men had knocked the girls out and was lying in wait to take out Cal.

Cal hesitated. He didn't have any paranormal abilities, so if one of Bly's guys was going to jump out and zap him with negative energy, he'd be a goner. But if that were the case, Belladonna wouldn't have led him straight into a trap. He crouched down to get a better look at the girls. He didn't see any injuries or blood. The sisters looked as though they were sleeping, but surely they wouldn't have just lain down to take a nap. Belladonna's cries would have roused them.

"*Meow!*" Belladonna batted something toward him. A tiny rib cage. A bird's rib cage.

A canary! Belladonna was trying to tell him the air was toxic. Like the canaries in the coal mines, this bird was probably brought in by the pirates to test for pockets of carbon monoxide or other gases that were not breathable. And this particular tunnel slanted downward—if the gas was heavier than air, it would accumulate down there, and no one at the upper level would be affected.

Cal didn't know what the gas was or whether it was naturally occurring or part of the elaborate booby traps he'd heard about, but he knew one thing—breathing too much of it might be deadly.

Cal didn't have any time to waste.

He stepped back and filled his lungs with untainted air then rushed toward the girls. Grabbing Celeste's and Morgan's arms, he dragged them up to the highest level, took another deep breath, and rushed back for Jolene and Fiona.

When they were out, he knelt by Celeste, his heart sinking. Her face was pale, her lips almost blue. He tapped her cheek. "Celeste, wake up!"

Relief flooded through him when her eyelids fluttered. "Are you okay?"

She nodded, then her eyes widened, and she jerked into a sitting position. "My sisters!"

Jolene, Morgan, and Fiona were all stirring. They sat up, coughing and sputtering.

"What happened?" Morgan asked.

"A booby trap!" Jolene said.

"Maybe." Cal helped Celeste to her feet then reached to do the same for Fiona. "It might be natural gas, but either way, you guys need to get out into the fresh air. Can you walk?"

They managed to get up and, leaning on each other, made their way, still coughing and sputtering, out of the tunnel. They attached the ropes for safety, and with Cal's help, they climbed up to the area outside the treasure pit and collapsed on the grass.

"What happened in there?" Jolene asked.

"I'm not sure. It might've been one of the booby traps," Cal said. "I think it was some kind of a gas or something like carbon monoxide. It knocked you out."

"I wonder if that's what happened to the skeleton. Poor guy got a booby-trapped steel trap on his foot and the gas," Morgan said.

"Belladonna was trying to warn us. That's why she was playing with the bones—to warn us off, not lure us in." Celeste scooped the cat into her lap and cuddled her. "Good girl."

"She came running out of the tunnel like a bat out of hell." Cal reached over and petted Belladonna's head, feeling the vibration of her loud purr. "That's how I knew something was wrong."

"Lucky thing, or we could have been in real trouble..." Celeste's words faded as the sounds of someone in the woods behind them captured their attention. They all turned to see Gordy burst from the woods. He stopped short in front of them.

"What are you guys doing lying around? Why didn't you answer?"

"What? We were in the cave, and there was a—"

"Never mind about that." He cut Jolene off. His face was grim, his eyes darting around as if he were expecting more people to burst out of the woods behind him. "I've been trying to call you. Buzz saw smoke over on the north side. Someone else is on the island."

CHAPTER SIX

*C*eleste's heart sank, and she stared at Gordy. *Had Dr. Bly's people found them already?*

"How many?" Luke's voice crackled over Gordy's walkie-talkie, and Gordy brought it up to his mouth. "Not sure. We saw the smoke from a fire. Looks like they are camped out on the north end of the island. Buzz is on his way down to scope it out now."

"Did you see any boats come to the island? Anything at the dock or moored offshore?" Luke asked.

"Negative."

"Have you alerted Cal and the girls?"

Gordy's gaze shifted to Celeste and her sisters, who were now standing and brushing off their jeans. "Yep. We're all together here now."

"We're clearing out down here. Meet you at the cabins pronto to formulate a plan."

"Okay. See you there."

Gordy turned his attention back to the group. "You guys coming?"

"Maybe you girls should rest," Cal said then turned to explain to Gordy. "We ran into some kind of fumes in the cave that knocked them out."

Gordy's rough gaze softened with concern. "Fumes?"

"Like carbon monoxide or something. I don't know if they're fit for—"

"We'll be fine," Jolene cut in. "I feel fine. Don't you guys?" She looked at her sisters, who all nodded.

"We need to come with you in case the people are paranormals." Fiona picked up a few more pebbles and loaded her pockets. "You'll need us to help fight them."

Some of us can help fight them, Celeste thought. But she wasn't going to dwell on that. She could still do a mean high karate kick that would render even a paranormal useless as long as she could place it before she was taken out by an energy strike. She'd do her best to help.

They made the short walk to the cabins and changed into gear more fitting for an altercation in the dense Nova Scotia forest. Camouflage shirts and pants. Various weapons. And, of course, their obsidian amulets to protect against negative energy.

Luke and Jake joined with a preliminary report from Buzz.

"Buzz said he only spotted one person moving around the fire. He couldn't get close enough to see the person, and they kept to some sort of cave that's down there. There could be others in the cave, or they might be in the woods, watching, so keep alert out there."

"Do we know if there are others?" Morgan asked. "Bly usually sends a crew."

"Probably," Luke said. "What's your feeling on it? Do you have a gut feeling on how many are here?"

Everyone had learned to respect Morgan's gut feelings, which had helped them on several occasions. But not this time. Morgan simply shook her head. "I got nothing."

"Well, I guess we have to go down and find out the old-fashioned way." Luke pulled out a map of the island and spread it on the picnic tables. "I think we should surround them. We need to split up, but I don't want to get too far away from each other. We might need to combine efforts to fight these guys."

Jolene pointed to several areas on the map. "Fiona and I can come from here, and Celeste and Morgan from there. Then between you, Jake, Cal, and Buzz, you can fill in around."

"Good thinking." Jake nodded at Jolene. "We can use the walkie-talkies to communicate for part of the way. Keep your voices low, though. Once we get within hearing range, we'll need to go to silence so as not to give ourselves away."

They made their way into the woods. Celeste stuck close to Morgan. The smell of crisp fallen leaves mingled with the salty ocean air as they traversed the dense woods, stepping over fallen branches and gnarled roots that stuck up from the ground. The large oaks and maples hadn't yet given up all their red-and-orange foliage, and their sun-dappled leaves created flickering shadows on the carpet of pinecones and acorns that covered the forest floor. Celeste brushed against a low bough of a fir tree, and the holiday scent of pine filled the air. They kept a slow but steady pace, not wanting the snapping of twigs or rustling of under-brush to alert anyone to their presence.

"Do you think it's Bly's people?" Celeste whispered. "Are you getting any sense of whether there are other paranormals, or people with bad intent?"

Morgan shook her head. "No. It's the weirdest thing. I'm not feeling apprehensive at all."

Celeste's stomach twisted. Morgan usually got gut feelings about enemy paranormals. Was something on the island messing with her gifts? And, if so, would it affect her other sisters' gifts too? Fiona had mentioned that Dubonnet might have amped-up skills that ghosts wouldn't normally have because of all the rock energy inside the tunnels. Maybe being inside the tunnels altered her sisters' paranormal skills too, but not in a good way. But they weren't *inside* a tunnel now.

Morgan paused, holding her arm out to stop Celeste. She brought her finger to her lips then crouched down and pointed. "Look, there's the fire."

Celeste tilted her head to follow Morgan's line of sight. Farther down the hill, about three hundred feet away, she could see gray wisps of smoke curling up in into the air. Her nerves tingled. They were about to meet the enemy.

Celeste stood and flexed her muscles. She might not be able to bend energy or turn rocks into flaming projectiles, but she could bust out a mean karate kick, and if that was what she had to do to help fight these guys, then that was what she would do.

Morgan stood and looked at her watch. They'd synchronized with the others earlier so they could converge on the area at exactly the same time. "We have three minutes, just about perfect timing to get there."

They continued slowly toward the fire, hypervigilant now for anyone else in the woods. If these people were any good, they would probably have lookouts stationed out here. Celeste's stomach tightened into a knot. The others were moving toward the fire too, and so far, she'd not heard anyone cry out. No sounds of fighting or gunfire. But still, she wondered, would she and Morgan get to the fire only to find out the others had already been captured?

And then they were there, standing cautiously just inside the woods, peeking through the branches at the fire. Oddly enough, the campsite appeared to be empty. There was no tent or other gear as she'd expected. Just a pair of jeans and a red plaid flannel shirt hanging on a makeshift clothesline.

What was up with that?

About twenty feet away, Fiona and Jolene appeared at the edge of the woods. Then Luke, Jake, Gordy, Buzz, and Cal could be seen in various spots surrounding the fire.

A movement at one end of the campsite caught her attention. The rocks had formed an outcropping that made a shelter about five feet high, and a figure was stirring inside. She could barely make out a head of dark hair. Her muscles tensed. She glanced around. Everyone else was also poised for action, awaiting Luke's signal.

Was there only one person here?

Luke must have thought so. He stepped into the clearing. His gun drawn, he walked silently up to the fire. The bad guy still had his back to them, but now she could see more of him. Tall, olive skin, broad shoulders, and a head of thick, dark, curly hair.

"Hands up, and turn around slowly," Luke commanded, though Celeste could hardly see how the guy could be armed since he was only wearing a pair of red boxer shorts.

As he put his hands up and slowly started to turn, a flicker of recognition ran through Celeste.

"Matteo?"

* * *

"WHAT ARE *YOU* DOING HERE?" Jolene's words sounded harsh, but Celeste noticed the look of softness in her eyes. Say what she might, Jolene was glad to see Matteo. She also noticed Jolene checking out his long, lean body, especially since he was only in his underwear.

"And why are you in your underwear?" Luke asked, putting his gun away.

Matteo's face spread into a sheepish grin as he grabbed the plaid shirt from the makeshift clothesline. "Dorian filled me in on the mission. She had me looking into where Bly's guys went with what they thought was the clue they got from the basement of that store. Once I did that, I figured you'd need my help, so I came right out."

Jolene looked at him suspiciously. "Oh really? Then how come you're lurking around down here without your clothes on?"

Matteo buttoned the shirt. "There was a naval training exercise off the coast here. I hooked up with one of the submersibles, but the island is too rocky to land on, so I had to hop out twenty feet away and swim."

"Swim?" Fiona glanced out at the cold grayish-blue waves. "It's freezing out there."

Matteo shrugged. "Hey, when you guys need my help, I come no matter what." He glanced tentatively at Jolene, who looked away quickly.

Celeste didn't know what was going on with her sister and Matteo, but she had a sneaking suspicion Jolene didn't want to admit she had true feelings for the tall, dark, and mysterious man. She might even be nervous that Matteo didn't return them. Maybe Celeste could whip up a spell to help her sister realize her true feelings. It was obvious Matteo was smitten with Jolene, and Celeste had long felt the two of them were meant for each other.

Matteo gestured toward the jeans still hanging on the line. "I got all wet swimming, so I was just drying off my stuff before I came up to meet with you guys. So what's going on?"

They sat in a circle around the fire and got down to business, filling Matteo in on everything they had discovered so far, including Celeste's conversation with Mirabella and their venture into the treasure pit. When Matteo heard about the mysterious gases inside the treasure pit, his eyes became filled with concern, and he reached out toward Jolene, squeezing her hand.

"I'm glad you guys made it out of there safely. Maybe we should take extra caution inside. I have heard those tunnels are booby-trapped."

"*Meow.*" Belladonna rubbed her face against Matteo's ankle.

He smiled and reached down to pet her. "Yeah, you tried to warn them, didn't you?"

"*Mew.*" Belladonna looked up at him and nodded.

"But what about Bly's guys?" Luke asked. "What did you find out about them?"

"They're still following a false lead from the box they got out of the basement of that store. They're in the Bahamas right now, but it's only a matter of time before they figure out they got the wrong box and get wind of your trip out here," Matteo said.

"All the more reason for us to take advantage of the uninterrupted time we have on the island," Jake said.

"I say we get back to camp and get Matteo set up in one of the cabins"—Luke flicked his gaze over to Jolene, who scowled—"or one of the tents. And then let's make a plan for early tomorrow morning."

Matteo grabbed his pants from the line and stepped into them. "Sounds good. Do you already have a game plan for tomorrow?"

"Not yet. What did you find down at the cove?" Morgan sat beside Luke, her arm linked through his.

"We saw some underwater caverns. Could be something to check out, but you need scuba gear to get in there, so it doesn't seem likely to be where the treasure is," Luke said.

"Why not? The sea level has risen since Mirabella's time," Cal said.

"And it's possible the pirates used underwater entrances on purpose," Matteo said. "Harder to get to."

"Well, we didn't see any quartz line in there," Jake said. "The sea level hasn't risen that far. I think it's more likely that the caverns are part of the system that floods the tunnels."

"I'd like to get farther into that tunnel that we accessed from the treasure pit," Celeste said. "Even though we didn't see the quartz line Mirabella told me about, the tunnel systems are all different now from when Mirabella was there. New passages have been dug, and I feel like we should explore more into the depths."

Cal's eyes narrowed. "It seems dangerous in there. Someone might have rigged that entrance recently, and we don't know what else we'll find."

"I don't think so," Jolene said. "I didn't detect any recent negative energy, and Jason said no one has been on the island."

"Maybe it was Dubonnet's ghost," Fiona said.

Matteo's left brow shot up. "Ghost?"

"Apparently, some old pirate ghost is haunting the island, trying to stop people from getting the treasure," Jake said.

"Is that the source of all these fatal accidents?" Matteo asked.

"I doubt it," Luke said, then after seeing Celeste's frown, he added, "Maybe some of them, but I'm sure many of them had to do with living beings, probably paranormals that were after the relic themselves and trying to scare off treasure hunters who might find it by accident and not realize it was anything special."

Jake nodded. "If one of them did, that relic could be hidden away in a private collection, and we'd never find it."

"I vote we continue in the tunnel. If we steer clear of the section that has the gas and proceed cautiously, I think we'll be okay." Celeste didn't have the same talent for reading auras as Jolene did or the amped-up intuition that Morgan did, but she *felt* that they'd been close to something important inside that tunnel. And one thing she did have was the ability to communicate with ghosts. If Dubonnet was in there, she'd at least be able to spot him and try to avoid anything he might lay out for a trap. Unlike previous treasure hunters who couldn't see ghosts, Celeste would be able to see him doing sneaky stuff right in front of them.

"I agree," Fiona said. "We need to check everything out thoroughly, and so far, that seems like the best course unless Cal has come up with something from the code on the rocks."

Cal shook his head. "I'm trying some new ciphers

out. Even if I do, though, we're probably still going to need to find the missing piece of rock."

"We're doing a search for that while we stand guard to make sure no one approaches the island," Buzz said.

"Okay, then I guess that settles it," Luke said. "We'll split up again. We'll start a methodical search, starting at the peak of the island and working our way down to look for the missing rock. That could take days, so meanwhile, some of us will take a closer look at the cove, and some will continue down the tunnel."

"Great. Let's get back to the cabins and rustle up some chow." Gordy kicked down the fire and spread sand on it. "Me and Buzz gotta get back to our lookout spot in case anyone else comes to the island."

"Yeah," Buzz said. "Hopefully if they do, they won't be using submersibles—there's no way we could see those."

"Let's hope we can find the relic and get out of here before anyone else comes." Luke started toward the woods. "I want to get an early start tomorrow so we can get as much done as possible before we have to deal with more than just a three-hundred-year-old ghost trying to sabotage our mission."

CHAPTER SEVEN

*T*he next morning, Celeste and her sisters went into the tunnel again, this time steering clear of the section where they'd succumbed to the mysterious gas the day before. The farther they went, the damper the air became. The dank, salty smell of seaweed permeated the tunnel, and the floor became slippery.

"No wonder Belladonna didn't want to come," Morgan said. "She hates wet floors."

"Yeah, she's a prima donna." Fiona flashed her light on the sides of the tunnel, revealing fissures where water seeped out. "But maybe she's smarter than us. Maybe she knows there's nothing in here. I don't see any white quartz."

"It might be farther down." Something at the periphery of Celeste's vision caught her eye.

What was that?

She whipped her head around in time to see what she thought was a misty swirl disappear into the dark. A ghost? Dubonnet? Or had Belladonna followed them in after all? No, it wasn't Belladonna. She wouldn't be ducking out of the way. She'd just trot right up to them.

Celeste wished it was a ghost, but not Dubonnet. She wished it was Mirabella. The one thing she could contribute to the mission was the information Mirabella had given her, but it wasn't proving to be very useful. She'd gone to the cliff the night before, hoping to get some better directions as to where to find this quartz line, but Mirabella wasn't there.

But if Mirabella had told her the truth, she wouldn't be down here in the tunnels, because she'd said she never left the cliff where Constantine was buried. Which left only one person. Dubonnet. A chill ran up Celeste's spine, and she peered farther into the tunnel. If a ghost had been there, it was gone now. Maybe it had been her imagination.

"So what's up with you and Matteo?" Morgan, apparently unaware of Celeste's ghost sighting, asked, eliciting an eye roll from Jolene.

"Nothing," Jolene said. "Just because I saved his life doesn't mean he owns me."

"I don't think he feels like he owns you," Fiona said. "I just think he wants to be with you."

"Sure he does. How come, before, he would just randomly show up, and now he seems to be around all the time?" Jolene asked. "I think he's reading more into this life-saving thing than necessary."

"Or maybe he figured out he wants to be around more. It happens," Morgan said. "Look at Cal and Celeste. Or me and Luke, for that matter."

"Whatever." Jolene jerked her flashlight along the walls and ceiling of the tunnel. "I decide who I want to be with, not some stupid old wives' tale. You guys should be looking for this line of quartz instead of interrogating me."

Celeste smiled, remembering the charm she'd cast the night before. She'd snuck out of her cabin and gathered some moss and acorn caps. She'd crushed them up and spread them in a line between Matteo's tent and Jolene's cabin right when the moon was at its highest. A little connection charm couldn't hurt. She knew her sister loved Matteo, and it was her own foolish stubbornness that was keeping them apart.

Something cold brushed against her arm, and Celeste spun around, shining the light back behind her. Nothing.

Was Dubonnet messing around with her, or was she just being paranoid?

Her hand snuck into her pocket. When she'd been gathering the moss and acorns for Jolene's charm, she'd also collected some ocean sand from the crevices of the rocks near the ocean and scraped some lichen from the granite boulders on the way. She could use them in a protective spell should they run into trouble here in the tunnel. She didn't know if the spell would work, but at least she could try. Now, given the way she was feeling, she was glad she had at least something to try to safeguard them from the ghost.

"Did you see something back there, Celeste?" Morgan asked.

"Oh, no. I was just looking at the rocks, double-checking if there was any quartz. I don't see any."

"Not back there, but look at this!" Fiona's light flashed on a streak of white on the side of the tunnel. She laid her palm on it, and a faint yellow glow flickered, as if someone were shining a light from inside. "This is it. The quartz line!"

"But it's not parallel. It goes up through the ceiling of the tunnel." Celeste's voice was laced with disappointment. "Mirabella said to follow it to the junction of three tunnels."

"Maybe she accessed it from another tunnel above this one," Morgan said. "This line could go upward then level off. The rocks in this area are at all kinds of angles. We should definitely check this out."

Celeste laid her palm on the side of the tunnel. Here, the layers of rock were almost vertical. They'd been heaved up long ago when the earth was being formed, but she knew that in other parts of the tunnels, the layers were horizontal. "But how? It goes up to the ceiling, and even though the layers might be horizontal farther up, I'm not sure digging is a good idea."

"I did bring tools." Jolene lifted a small pickax from her belt, which Celeste saw also contained a chisel.

"We won't need them. Look." Morgan had moved farther down the tunnel and was shining her light on an opening in the wall. There was a thin crack, beyond which another tunnel angled upwards.

Fiona stood back as far as she could, angling her light on the opening and the quartz line. "That passage looks like it slopes up at a thirty-degree angle. If that's the case and this quartz vein continues at its current trajectory, then they should intersect up the line somewhere."

"We should go in." Jolene started, but Morgan pulled her back.

"Wait. Luke said we should only explore the main tunnel," Morgan said.

Jolene scowled. "Since when do you do exactly as Luke says?"

"Good point." Morgan let go of Jolene's arm. Jolene slipped into the tunnel, and Morgan followed.

"We'll just go a little ways in and see if we can find the quartz line, then we'll report back to the guys," Jolene called over her shoulder.

"Sounds good." Fiona slipped in after Morgan.

Celeste glanced uneasily behind her. She didn't see any sign of a ghost, but just in case, she pulled the sand and lichen from her pocket and trotted a few feet farther down into the unexplored part of the tunnel. That was the direction she'd seen Dubonnet's ghost swirling in. She sprinkled the sand and lichen from one side of the tunnel to the other in a thin line while mumbling the protective spell that would hopefully stop Dubonnet's ghost from coming in behind them. She wasn't sure if she'd even seen his ghost, but if she had, she was sure he was hanging out deeper into the tunnel system, and this would hopefully keep him back there. She turned and jogged back up the tunnel to catch up with her sisters.

"Where were you?" Fiona flashed her light on Celeste as she trotted up to them.

"Just checking something out."

Morgan frowned. "Is something wrong back there?"

"I don't think so. Just making sure."

Morgan nodded, and they continued on a few feet before Fiona stopped them.

"Look. Here's the quartz line." Fiona flashed her light onto the wall, and they followed the faint, thin white line of quartz, which angled up more steeply than the slope of the tunnel. The tunnel narrowed until they had to walk single file.

"I don't know about this, guys," Celeste said. "It's getting pretty narrow."

"Just a few more feet, then we'll turn back." Their shoulders were almost scraping the sides now, and Celeste felt the raw edges of claustrophobic panic clutch at her.

Suddenly, Morgan stopped, and they almost rammed into her.

"Check this out." She took one step and moved to the side, flashing her light around so that the others could see that the narrow tunnel had opened into a huge cavern. It must've been ten feet wide and twenty feet long. The ceiling arched several feet above them.

"What is this place?" They moved into the cavern, shining their lights all around the walls.

"There are tool marks on the walls. I think this is man-made," Jolene said.

Celeste inspected the walls, rubbing her fingertips over the sharp edges where tools had cut away the rock. Someone had carved this room out, but for what purpose? Could this be where the pirates had hidden the treasure, and if so, was this where Mirabella had hidden the relic?

Celeste spun around, flashing her light every-where. "I don't see the quartz vein, so I don't know if this is where Mirabella would've hidden the relic."

"They didn't dig this out for nothing. There must be something important in here. Maybe we should do a little exploring before we call the guys in," Jolene said.

"I don't know if that's such a good idea. There might be—"

Kaboom!

The explosion knocked Celeste against the wall. The sounds of falling rocks sparked panic in her chest, and she whirled around to see stones of all sizes— some the size of baseballs, others over a foot wide— falling in a pile in front of the narrow opening they'd come in through. She watched in horror as the rubble filled the entire opening in a split second. In a panic, she bounced her light off all the walls, desperately seeking a crack that would indicate an exit.

There were no other tunnels out.

They were trapped inside the cavern.

CHAPTER EIGHT

"**N**o!" Morgan dove for the entrance, dropping her flashlight in the process. It bounced on the floor, sending beams of light ping-ponging around the cavern like a crazy strobe light.

"Morgan!" Jolene lunged for Morgan, pulling her back to stop her from becoming injured by the falling rocks.

Celeste's pulse thudded as they stood staring at each other, riding out the aftershock of the explosion. After a few seconds, the rocks stopped falling. Jolene let go of Morgan, who retrieved her flashlight and waved the beam around the cavern.

"We're trapped in here," Fiona said.

"We don't know that yet. Maybe we can dig out." Jolene walked to the blocked entrance, shoved her small flashlight in her back pocket, and stretched to reach the top of the pile. She tugged carefully on a baseball-sized rock. She dislodged it, and two smaller rocks took its place.

"Be careful! Those could cave in and crush you," Morgan said.

"Wait a minute. Let me check this out." Fiona approached the pile of rocks slowly, holding her palms out in front of her. She closed her eyes and ran her fingers over the rocks, nodding and humming as she did. Some of the rocks glowed subtly as her fingers passed over them.

"Well?" Morgan asked.

"The wall isn't that thick," Fiona said. "But we need to be careful. We don't want to cause these heavy rocks to come in and bury us. We'll start at the top and pull out the smaller rocks first, letting things settle slowly." Fiona pulled out a small pebble, then another.

The others joined her, carefully pulling out the smaller rocks and letting the wall shift slowly downward, careful not to disturb it in such a way that it caved in toward them.

"What caused that, anyway?" Morgan asked.

"Some kind of explosion," Jolene said.

"Do you think it could have been one of the booby traps?" Celeste asked.

"Either that, or someone caused it on purpose," Jolene answered.

"Which means someone besides us is here."

Morgan twisted her lips. "But if they were, Gordy and Buzz would have seen them, wouldn't they?"

"Unless they were sneaky, or they took Gordy and Buzz out somehow," Jolene said.

"I hope the boys are okay up top." Fiona pulled out a large rock, and they all stood back while things settled.

"We'll head straight to them if we can," Morgan said. "Hopefully, the exit isn't blocked."

The threat of what might be happening aboveground caused them to pick up the pace. The pile was only a foot thick, and soon, they had dug out enough at the top so they could scramble over and into the narrow passage.

The girls hurried down the narrow path as quickly as they could.

"Wait a minute. What's that sound?" Jolene asked.

Celeste strained forward to hear what sounded like a hissing or a roaring. It was getting louder.

"I think that's rushing water!" Morgan's voice was tinged with panic, and they picked up the pace, rushing toward the opening that led to the main tunnel.

"It's filling with water!" Jolene rushed in, but the force of the water repelled her. "I don't think we can make it back to the entrance!"

Water rushed toward them quickly, soaking Celeste's feet and swirling around her ankles.

"This water must be from the bottom of the treasure pit! Whatever happened must have flooded that pit, and now it's rushing into the tunnel. We'll never get through. We have to turn around and find another way out!" Celeste pulled them back down the way they'd come, sloshing through the now ankle-deep water.

Celeste hadn't seen any other tunnels except the one with the mysterious gas, and they certainly weren't going in there. The only hope was to find something farther into the tunnel system than they'd already ventured.

She broke into a jog, the water now up to her knees, slowing her pace. Her feet felt wooden, numb from the ice-cold seawater, which was rising at an alarming rate.

When they got to the opening that led to the cavern, Celeste's heart skidded. The charm she'd placed a few feet farther down the tunnel to block any attack from Dubonnet's ghost had worked. It had created a barrier, but unfortunately, that barrier must also work on water, because they were met with a huge wave where the water pushed up against the invisible barrier and curled back toward them. Celeste tried to break through, but she couldn't. The force of the water was too strong.

'What's that?" Jolene yelled.

"I put a protective charm on the tunnel! We can't get through!"

"We need to go back this way!" Morgan tugged them toward the path that led to the cavern.

"No! There's no way out from there!" Celeste yelled.

"It's higher ground. Maybe we can wait it out until the water recedes," Morgan said. "This must be part of the booby-trap system set up to flood certain tunnels. We must have done something in that cavern to trip it. But it can't fill the whole thing to the top, can it?"

No one had an answer to that, so they turned and ran up the narrow tunnel, scrambling over the rocks into the cavern. Even here, the water was seeping in, and an inch of the floor was covered.

So much for higher ground.

"I don't know if this was such a good idea." Fiona's rubber-soled boots sloshed water around as she moved farther into the cavern. "What if the water doesn't recede?"

"It can't keep flooding in here forever. Eventually, gravity will take over, and the water will level off. And besides, we don't have much choice." Jolene started to stack the rocks, pulling more from the rubble at the entrance and making a platform. "Besides, I have an idea. Help me with these rocks."

Amidst the rising water, the sisters grabbed rocks and started adding to the pile. Celeste's fingers were numb from dipping into the cold water, but seeing as the water had now risen to her knees and she didn't have a better idea, she worked as fast as she could.

"What's your idea?" Fiona had migrated to the sides of the cavern and was running her hands along the walls, probably hoping to find a section that ran alongside another tunnel close enough to dig through, Celeste guessed.

"The tunnel to the cavern slopes upward, which means the cavern is higher than the entrance, but it's only a few hundred feet away from it. Up top, the ground is pretty much level, which means the top of the cavern is probably pretty close the surface." Jolene climbed up to the top of the platform and pulled the pickax out of her belt. "I figure if we can chisel out enough of the rock, then maybe we can get out that way."

Celeste's gaze flicked up to the top of the cavern. "You mean if we dig up through the top of the cavern, we would come out on that flat grassy area near the treasure-pit hole we came in on?"

"Maybe. The trick is to do it without caving the whole top in." Jolene swung at a piece of rock, which crumbled and splashed into the water.

"Too bad at this rate, the water will reach the ceiling before we can get out," Morgan said.

"Maybe I can help." Fiona climbed up beside Jolene and placed her palm on the rocks, eliciting a faint glow. "If I heat the rocks, they aren't as brittle, so it might go faster."

Jolene swung again, and a bigger chunk fell out.

"You're going to have to go a *lot* faster." Morgan stood waist deep in the water as she fished for more stones to make the platform big enough for all of them to stand on. "This is filling up quickly."

"Maybe I can help." Celeste's heart tumbled at the idea. Her last spell had worked, with the unfortunate unintended consequence of creating the wave barrier, but maybe this one could buy them some time without any adverse effects. She closed her eyes and plunged her hands into the water, cupping them together and bringing up a handful of water, which she let trickle through her fingers.

She reached deep into her heart and whispered:

By WATER, *Earth, Air, and Fire,*
  I ask thee now, grant my desire,
  Evaporate quick as can be
  This charm is done, so mote it be

THE FOUR OF them were silent, watching the water trickle out of Celeste's hands. Celeste didn't know what she expected. She'd hoped the water might evaporate and the level would go down, but it didn't.

"Nothing happened. Sorry," she said.

"No, something happened!" Morgan pointed to the surface of the water. In the cavern, with only their headlamps and handheld lights to illuminate, the water looked as dark as midnight, and Celeste couldn't see anything happening.

"It's not rising as quickly," Fiona said.

"And look, it's forming condensation on the ceiling." Jolene chipped away with the pickax. "That's making the rocks fall off faster. If we can get close to the surface, then maybe I can send some energy up that will blast a hole in it. I don't dare do that now for fear the whole thing will cave in on us, but if we could carve out a small area that was near the layer of earth on top, I think it could work."

They stacked the rest of the rocks, and everyone piled up near Jolene to help. Fiona kept her palm on the rocks, Morgan held a flashlight, and Celeste took a chisel and started to pry around the edges where Jolene was picking.

"What's that?" Fiona held her hand out, and they all stopped what they were doing. "I think I hear a cat."

"Belladonna?" Celeste looked around in panic. "She couldn't have gotten in here."

"No." Fiona shook her head and pointed to the top of the cavern. "I think she's outside. Listen."

Celeste cocked her ear toward the ceiling and

heard a faint muffled sound. A meow. And scratching. "I think she's trying to dig us out!"

"We must be close to the surface!" Jolene swung the pickax harder.

"Good thing." Morgan's face turned grim as she looked down, and Celeste realized the water had risen to her waist. Though the sides and top of the cavern were dripping with condensation now, the rising water was starting to outpace the amount of condensation. As usual, her spell hadn't been good enough.

Celeste worked the chisel harder. They were so close.

The water inched past her waist to her chest.

She dug faster.

Ka-pling!

"What was that?"

Celeste rammed her chisel into the rock again, feeling less resistance than normal. "Something's behind here! I might have reached the top!"

Jolene shifted positions with Fiona to get a better angle at the area Celeste had uncovered. She swung her pickax at the area, and a large chunk of rock splashed into the water. Hope bloomed in Celeste's chest, and she looked up, expecting to see blue sky or at least dirt indicating they'd dug to the soft ground above, but all she saw was a dark hole.

"It's some kind of chamber." Celeste stuck her hand into the space. It was only about a foot wide and a foot deep. Toward the back, her fingers met with cold, hard metal. "What the—"

She pulled the object out.

Golden light sparkled off the small dome-shaped object in her hand. It was small—no more than six inches long and four inches wide—but ornate, with an etched design and glittery cobalt-blue gems on each side.

"What is that?" Fiona stared at the box.

Though the icy water was now reaching Celeste's shoulders, she was mesmerized by the object, holding it above water for them to see. "It's a jewelry box. The relic must be inside."

"Open it," Morgan said.

"We don't have time for that!" Jolene yelled as she swung the axe rapidly. "We can look in it later."

But Celeste wasn't listening. She held the box carefully in one hand while the numb fingers of her other hand fumbled with the clasp on the front.

The water inched higher, and the chill of it stole the air from Celeste's lungs. She couldn't feel her fingers, much less get them to work the clasp.

"I think we're almost there!" Jolene swung the pickax with all her might, jumping up to add force to the swing.

She landed hard on the pile of rocks, and the ones below them shifted.

Celeste pitched forward, almost falling headfirst

into the water. Her grip on the box loosened, and it tumbled out of her hand.

"No!" Celeste watched in horror as it was swallowed up in the dark liquid depths.

Morgan grabbed her upper arm just as she was about to jump in after it. "You'll never find it down there!"

"I can't just let it slip away!" Her teeth were chattering, the words coming out choppy.

"We'll come in later with scuba gear. We have to get out." Morgan could barely open her mouth because the water was up past her chin. Her lips were purple.

She had a point. What good would it do to have the relic if they drowned in this damn cavern?

But would they be able to get out? Celeste jerked her eyes upward to see Jolene still trying to chip away at that one section. But now, with the water up past her chin, she didn't have much momentum. And even worse, this part of the cavern was arched, so there was less surface area now, and the water level was rising even faster.

"I think we're close. I'm going to try zapping some energy up!" Jolene raised her hands up toward the ceiling. Sparks of energy crackled and popped on the wet surface of her palms.

The water reached the bottom of Celeste's nostrils, and she tilted her chin up so she could breathe. A few more minutes, and they would be totally submerged.

Celeste rolled her eyes toward Jolene. *Why wasn't there any energy coming out of her palms?*

"It's not working. I'm practically frozen..." Jolene stabbed her palms up toward the ceiling again, and Celeste saw an orange glow zip through the cracks of the rock above right before the water flooded over her face. She closed her eyes. The tip of her nose was now the only thing above water, and she took one last, deep breath, letting herself relax and succumb to the sleepy chill of the icy ocean water.

CHAPTER NINE

$\mathcal{C}$eleste must have gotten past the point of feeling the icy cold. She didn't feel any pain, just a sense of peace. She was incredibly sleepy, her mind letting go of all her concerns one by one as she drifted in weightless suspension. The sensation of floating there in the pitch-dark cavern was actually kind of comfortable.

And then something latched onto her arm with a painful viselike grip, and she was ripped through the water. It was like leaving a comfortable cocoon. She didn't want to go. She kicked and jerked, but whatever it was that had ahold of her was stronger.

And then she burst out of the water, the cool air hitting her like a glacier, and her back collided with the hard ground.

She heaved in a breath of air and choked out a lungful of water.

She saw sweet blue sky. And green grass. And what was that warm, sandpapery thing rubbing her cheek?

"*Meow.*"

"Belladonna!" Celeste rolled on her side, coughing as she petted the cat. Belladonna submitted to a few ear rubs then trotted off toward the other Blackmoore sisters, whom Celeste was relieved to see were all lying on the grass, in various stages of recovery. Her previous apathy about her watery death evaporated, and her eyes sought out Cal. She was grateful and overjoyed to be alive.

"Is everyone all right?" Jolene was on her knees, her long, wet hair dripping on the ground. Matteo crouched beside her, rubbing her back. Jolene leaned into Matteo for support, and Celeste's heart swelled. Maybe the connection charm had actually worked.

Then disappointment settled in. That *charm* might have worked, but her magic still wasn't helping with their mission. The spell she'd cast to deflect Dubonnet had practically gotten them killed, and worse, she'd had the relic right in her hands and lost it.

"I'm fine," Celeste said as Cal rushed over to her.

"I'm good." Morgan let Luke help her up.

"Me too." Fiona smiled up at Jake, who was hovering around her with a concerned look on his face.

"What happened?" Cal helped Celeste up, pulled her close, then held her at arm's length, apparently checking for damage.

"Something blew up in there and caused a cave-in. We were trapped inside, and then water started rushing in." Jolene wrung the water out of her hair.

"We heard the explosion. Matteo was here first. I saw him reach into the ground and pull Jolene out, then Luke and I helped get the rest of you out. But how in the world did you get in there?" Jake pointed to the black hole of the cavern. The water was level with the top.

"We might have triggered one of the booby traps in there." Jolene glanced at the black hole. "It's a cavern. Man-made. But I knew the top of it was close to the surface, and when the water rushed in, we didn't have much choice but to dig up."

"Luckily, Jolene's calculations were right. But how did Matteo know we were under there? The last thing I remember is that we couldn't punch through before the water swallowed us." Morgan shivered, and Luke pulled her tighter.

"You did break through," Matteo said. "I heard the explosion and was running for the treasure pit. That whole entrance is underwater now. Then I saw red-energy arcs coming out of the ground and ran over in time to see a hole open up." Matteo looked at Jolene. "I knew you were inside, and I was going to jump in, but I could see you just under the water and pulled you all out."

"Thanks for that," Jolene said. "We thought we were close to the surface and were trying to dig out."

"So Matteo saved Jolene?" Morgan's lips quirked. "Sounds like that might make them even."

Matteo smiled, but Jolene frowned and moved away from him. So much for the connection spell.

"What made you guys dig right there?" Luke pointed to the patch of ground. Claw marks where Belladonna had been scratching her way down toward them could still be seen at the edges of the hole.

"I thought I heard Belladonna." Jolene looked down at the white cat, which weaved figure eights around her ankles.

"Guess we did hear her." Morgan squatted to pet the cat.

"But what I don't understand is *why* would there be an explosion? If you triggered something that opened the flood chambers, would there actually be an explosion? Was it gunpowder rigged by some pirate three hundred years ago?" Jake asked.

"Good question," Luke said. "But whatever happened, we won't be able to continue our search here until the waters recede. Unless we dive, but that's dangerous and won't be nearly as easy."

"Actually, we won't have to keep searching," Morgan said.

Luke's brows quirked up. "Oh?"

"We found the relic." Morgan pointed to the hole in the ground, which now had water bubbling out of it. "It's in there."

"*Was* in there," Celeste corrected. "It might have been washed out in the current at the bottom."

"That's great news! We can dive in and look for it." Luke glanced over at the hole. "Seems like the water has leveled off. If it doesn't recede too rapidly, there won't be much of a current, and we can simply dive in and get it. Hopefully, it will still be near where you dropped it."

"Hopefully." Celeste's shoulders sagged as Cal wrapped his sweatshirt around her. "But I had it in my hands, and I lost it. Sorry, guys. I failed you."

"No, you didn't!" Morgan rushed to Celeste's side. "The rocks shifted, and it slipped out. Could have happened to anybody. Besides, you found the secret chamber it was stashed in. If you hadn't dug where you did, we would never even know it was there, and we'd waste a ton of time searching the rest of these tunnels."

Morgan's words did little to cheer Celeste. "Yeah, but—"

"What's going on? Are you guys okay? I heard an explosion up there." Buzz pointed to the west, where the island sloped upward, and Celeste noticed he had something in his hand.

"There was an explosion... or something. The flood

chambers opened and flooded the tunnel. But we're okay." Jolene's brows tugged together. "What's that in your hand?"

"I found this near where I thought the explosion was. Looks like a gun, but I've never seen this model."

"Let me see." Jolene turned the gun over in her hand then passed it to Morgan. "That's no regular gun. That's an energy gun like the ones Dr. Bly had when we rescued Mom. And if it's on this island, that can only mean one thing."

Morgan's face was grim as she passed the gun to Fiona. "We've got company."

CHAPTER TEN

"*C*an you show us where you found that?" Jolene asked.

"'Course. I was right over on the west side near a big outcropping of ledge," Buzz said.

"We should change first." Fiona pointed to her outfit. Soaking wet wasn't exactly conducive to hiking through the woods in the middle of fall.

They hightailed it to their cabins and changed in record time then followed Buzz into the woods.

The path to the outcropping was mercifully devoid of underbrush. Celeste was tired from their earlier adventure and didn't know if she could have weathered a hike that involved cutting away shrubs and jumping over logs. Since the hardwoods were sparse, the sun shone through, and its warming rays on Celeste's shoulders got rid of the remaining chill from the icy water. It was still Indian summer, and the temperatures were in the low seventies. The path led to a section of the island where large boulders were wedged between outcroppings of ledge.

"It was right down here." Buzz pointed to the ground in front of an enormous boulder wedged between an outcropping of ledge and several smaller boulders. "I was on the hill, looking for anyone approaching the island, and heard a loud bang. Then I felt the vibrations. When I looked around, I thought I saw something moving up here, so I ran up, but there was nothing. Just this gun. I picked it up and rushed down to make sure you guys were okay. That's when I found you all lying on the grass. Gordy is out scouring the island to see if he can find evidence of whoever belongs to this gun."

Luke turned toward the ocean and frowned. "How would someone get on the island without us seeing?"

Buzz shrugged. "We're watching constantly during the day and set up a camera at night, but if they came in without lights, I suppose someone could have landed."

"Sounds like that would be pretty dangerous," Jake said. "The entire perimeter of the island is rocks."

"Maybe they swam in like I did," Matteo suggested.

"Never mind that. Why would someone leave a paranormal-energy gun just lying up here?" Morgan asked.

Fiona stepped over to the rock wall. "I think I might know why. Something about these rocks reminds me of the cave-in in the cavern."

She ran her palm flat along the boulders. The area didn't have a pile of rubble like the cave-in in the cavern. It was just big boulders and ledge with a few smaller rocks.

Fiona ran her hands over the area between the boulder and the ledge where a few smaller pieces of rock had wedged between. Dust puffed out of the spaces in between, and a slight humming sound came from the rocks. As her palms passed over, a few sparks of light jumped out from the cracks.

She snapped her fist shut and turned to face them. "Something volatile happened to these rocks recently. The energy in the rocks is still vibrating from the movement. I think the ledge was blasted, then somehow it was fused to the boulders. It must have taken powerful energy to make this happen."

Celeste looked down at the gun. "You mean one of Bly's men used this gun to blast a hole in the ledge here? How would they know to do that? And why?"

"They must have suspected there was a tunnel just beyond the ledge," Luke said.

"But why would they seal themselves in?" Jolene asked.

"Maybe they didn't intend to seal themselves in. Maybe they just wanted to blast a hole in the rock,"

Celeste said. "That would explain why the gun was on the outside. Something must have happened, and the rocks opened, they jumped in, but then somehow the rocks fused back together. One of the guys must have dropped the gun. Maybe he got injured or something."

"So the real question is... what are they doing in there, or are they lying dead crushed under these rocks?" Matteo said.

Morgan stepped up to the rocks and closed her eyes, screwing them shut. "They're in there. I feel the vibes."

Jolene nodded. "I can see their energy trail. Blue and green with excitement, but somehow something went wrong. They must not have intended to cause whatever happened that blocked them in."

"And whatever they did caused the cave-in in the cavern and the flood chambers to be opened," Fiona said.

"Probably. It's still possible our digging around in the cavern caused the flooding. They might have had that booby-trapped. It makes sense they would want to protect what was in there. There might even be more treasure hidden there, and while I doubt that pirates other than Mirabella knew the value of the relic, they would want to protect the other treasure for its monetary value," Celeste said.

"We may never know if it was whatever Bly's guys did here or your digging that caused the flooding, but what I'd like to know is how did these guys get here, and what led them to this exact spot?" Jake asked.

"I know how they got here." Gordy pushed aside a pine bough and stepped into the group, his breath coming in short bursts. He bent at the waist, resting his palms on his knees. He thrust his chin out toward the ocean. "I found an inflatable. A Zodiac FC420 pulled up on the rocks down there along with a tent and camping gear."

"A 420?" Luke said. "That's pretty small. If they brought gear, that would mean there wouldn't be room for too many of them."

"There could only be two of them. There's no way it could fit three people and gear," Jake said.

"Good. At least we know we only have to battle two of them." Jolene smiled. "Should be easy peasy."

"Yeah, especially since we now have one of their guns." Morgan studied the gun in her hand. "We need to figure out how to use this thing."

"I remember seeing them use it before, and they simply slid this lever and then pulled the trigger like a real gun." Jolene pointed to a lever on the side and then the trigger.

"Be careful with that." Luke grabbed the gun from Morgan. "It's dangerous. It could be damaged and might backfire or something. I'll save it for Dorian, and she can have someone reverse-engineer it. In the meantime, maybe I should send her a message to see if she has any intel on why Bly's men picked this spot."

"And I think I know why they picked this spot." Cal peeked out from behind a large outcropping of ledge and motioned for them to join him.

They went to stand beside him, and he pointed at a jagged piece of ledge stuck up into the air. It was faintly chiseled with letters just like the rock they'd found in the box from LeBlanc's old store.

"I think this is the missing piece of rock that goes with the ones we have." Cal took out his cell phone and snapped a picture.

"Bly must've gotten a lead after all. It must have led them to this very spot. But how could they have solved the puzzle without the rest of the rocks?" Luke asked.

Cal, still frowning at the inscribed rock, rubbed his chin. "I don't think they could have. I think they might've gotten a lead to this piece of the puzzle and assumed the relic was right near it. They might not realize there is more of the puzzle to solve and that the relic is near here. But I don't think it is."

"Well, of course it isn't. I had the darn thing in my hand down in the cavern down there." Celeste pointed in the general direction of the cavern, which they couldn't see from their vantage point. "That's not anywhere near here."

"If Bly's guys are in there, do you think they know we're here on the island?" Jolene asked.

"I'm not sure." Matteo had come to stand close behind Jolene. She looked at him funny and then inched away as he continued talking. "When I did my intel, they were following up on the fake lead from that box they'd stolen from the store. None of them knew that you girls had been in the area, so they might not know we are here. As far as I know, they have no idea we are following a lead too."

"If they do know that we are here, they might be trying to get the relic out without us even noticing. With only two of them against all of us, they might not want to risk a battle. Even with those energy guns," Luke said. "Bly has intel too, you know, and it's pretty good."

"Either way, now they're stuck in there." Jake pointed to the rocks. "Which gives us a head start, so I say we get our scuba gear, dive into that cavern, retrieve the relic, and get the heck out of here before we have to cross paths with them."

"Well, that's the thing." Cal glanced from the inscription on the rock to the direction of the cavern. "I need my paper and pencil to do some calculations, but from what I'm seeing with this missing piece, I'm not sure the relic is where you guys think it is."

"We saw it there," Morgan said. "And besides, those rocks were etched three hundred years ago. Maybe things have changed on the island since."

"Or maybe you're wrong." Fiona shot Cal an apologetic look. "Either way, we know what we saw in that cavern, and we better get in there and extract it before Bly's guys figure out they are on a wild goose chase and come after us."

* * *

WHILE THE OTHERS headed to the cabins, Celeste stayed behind with Cal, who was still scratching his head and puzzling over the markings on the rock. She was curious as to why he was still puzzling over the rock when they already knew where the relic was.

"What's going on? You seem distracted by this rock, and we really don't need to decrypt the code anymore anyway," Celeste asked him.

Cal stepped back from the rock and pulled his cell phone out of his back pocket then navigated to earlier photos showing the other rocks as well as photos he'd taken of the notes he'd made while trying to decrypt the code.

"See these?" He pointed to the photos of the rocks. "The translation should be directions, steps we take to find the relic, right?"

Celeste nodded. "Yeah. So?"

"Well, these three pictures show all the inscriptions. Look at how many letters there are. It's not really enough for much direction."

Celeste frowned. There were sixteen letters and a

few other characters that looked as if they could be separators or some other type of code marker. "I guess it doesn't seem like a lot. Do you mean it's supposed to say something like 'fifty paces to the oak tree, turn right, and at thirty paces, x marks the spot'?"

"Something like that. At the very least, it should give directions to landmarks and where to go from there. But I don't see how it could possibly be much direction with so few letters. I thought the missing rock would have more letters on it."

"Maybe there is another rock?" Hadn't Mirabella said something about three large Scotch pines? There weren't any in the area, not even an old tree stump that would be large enough.

Cal looked at his photos again. "I don't think so. Look at the edges of the rocks—they all match up. It doesn't look like any more is missing."

He looked out over the ocean, his eyes cloudy. Obviously, his mind was on his calculations and not the view. Then he frowned and turned to her, his eyes filling with concern. He wrapped one of her curls around his finger. "Your hair is still wet. Are you warm enough? I don't want you catching a cold."

Celeste's heart warmed at his concern. He slipped his arm around her, and she snuggled into him.

"I'm fine. It's warm out. But if you're right about the code on the rocks, does it really matter? We don't need directions anymore, because I found that box."

Cal looked puzzled. "Box?"

"Yeah, I found a jeweled box in that cavern, and the relic must have been in it."

"So you didn't actually see the relic?"

"No. But it must have been in there. I mean, the box was all fancy and..." Celeste's words drifted off. The cavern had obviously been dug out by someone. She assumed pirates wanting to hide treasure. And that was why it filled up when the booby traps were set off, because it was full of treasure. Or at least one very important treasure.

"Where exactly was this cavern? I mean, was the path simple enough that the directions could be written with the few letters on these rocks?" Cal asked.

Celeste pressed her lips together. "Maybe. From the start of the treasure pit, we went straight down, took a right, then another right, and followed that to the cavern. But even if that route couldn't be mapped out with the letters on the rocks, it's possible Constantine accessed it through a different entry point."

Cal sighed. "I'm sure you're right and the relic was in there. We have to check it out either way. Hopefully, we can find it quickly. We don't know how long it'll be before Bly's men realize they're on the wrong track and come out after us."

"Now that you have the missing piece of rock, you can figure out exactly what it says, can't you?" Maybe it wouldn't be a bad idea to decode the clue that Constantine left just in case."

Cal pursed his lips. "Well, that's the thing. I could if I knew the cipher code. I've tried all the programs I know and even some sophisticated cipher keys that don't have software programs. I'm beginning to think this is a columnar transposition cipher."

"What's that mean?"

"It's trickier than a regular cipher. The key is three rows of letters that you line up in columns for the decryption. So you figure out what each letter means from those columns. Do you see what I mean?"

"I think so." Celeste vaguely remembered Cal explaining how to decrypt complicated codes to her. Maybe she should have paid attention to all his little lessons. She knew they had to look for patterns, and sometimes you could decrypt one message only to find that *that* was actually an encrypted message that needed another key to decrypt. But she didn't remember hearing him talk about this column thing before.

They started walking slowly back toward the cabins as Cal explained further. "In a regular cipher, you might have a number that correlates to a letter, or sometimes the key is hidden in a book or other text. That could still be the case here."

"Like that time we had to reference a certain word

in a certain paragraph in a book to break the code?" Celeste referred to one of their earlier missions.

"That's it exactly. In this case, though, it's not as simple as referencing a page, paragraph, and word. You need a whole bunch of words."

"Sounds complicated."

"That's what makes it fun. Though, so far, it's been more frustrating than fun. And, even if we recover the relic, I still want to decrypt it."

"I figured you would." Cal was the kind of guy that never left something half-finished. Celeste knew that once they recovered the relic, he'd still want to figure out the directions and follow them to make sure they were right. But his attention to detail and his dogged determination to see things through to the end was what made him valuable on their missions and one of the things she liked about him the best.

"Luckily, the message is short, so once I crack it, we'll be able to figure it out easily," Cal said.

"If anyone can do it, you can." Celeste grabbed Cal's hand and was rewarded with his charming smile.

"Thanks. But right now I think we need to get into that cavern and see what was in the box. I don't have the luxury of working on decrypting it right now. I think Luke is going to need my help."

"Why? Seems like a simple-enough dive, and he has plenty of people."

Cal glanced back at the ledge uncertainly. "I'm not

one to take chances. Like to have all my bases covered, and since it could take a while to recover that box, I think it would be smart to suggest to Luke that we have someone at the exits to warn us if the enemy is coming, which means he's going to need me to help with the dive."

ive minutes later, they exited the woods to find the others out in front of the cabins with various pieces of scuba gear spread out in front of them. Luke was already in his wetsuit. Jake was hoisting scuba tanks on his back. Gordy handed an underwater metal detector to Cal and clapped him on the shoulder as he brushed past.

"I'm sending Buzz up to guard the place where Bly's men went in. Matteo is on his way to guard the treasure pit, and Gordy is down at the cove, guarding the underwater cave exits. If Bly's men come out, I want to know about it," Luke said.

Celeste and Cal exchanged a look then knuckle-tapped. Sending someone to the exits had been exactly what they had just been talking about.

Luke frowned at them then pointed to a wetsuit.

"Suit up, Cal. The three of us will dive in. Hopefully, the metal detector will help speed up the recovery process."

"I'll dive too and show you where I dropped the box," Celeste said.

"No way. You girls were in the water too much today. I can't let you go back in there." Luke reached around behind his shoulder and tugged up the zipper on his wetsuit.

"What do you mean?" Anger and indignation simmered in Celeste's chest. She hated being told what to do, and it was her responsibility to retrieve that box. But then she realized why he didn't want her to go back in. She'd already screwed up once when she'd dropped the relic, and Luke probably didn't want to risk her screwing up again. She could hardly blame him. Maybe it was better if she left the retrieval to everyone else.

Fiona fisted her hands on her hips. "We're not just going to sit around here and do nothing while you guys dive."

"Of course you're not. You guys can split up. Two of you stay topside while we dive. We'll need tethers because it could be tricky inside there with the rubble you described. We need someone up above, ready to pull us out, not to mention someone to protect us if those two thugs of Bly's get past Gordy, Buzz, or Matteo and end up here. We're vulnerable down there, so it's an important job."

Luke's words seemed to mollify Fiona. Jolene not so much.

"So that's for two of us. What are the other two going to do?" Jolene asked.

"The other two can start packing. As soon as we come up with this relic, we are getting out of here. We don't know how long Bly's guys are going to be down in those tunnels, and we need to get off the island before they come back for us. In fact, I've already put a call in to Jason to come and get us," Luke said.

Morgan's ice-blue eyes turned downright frosty as she glared at Luke. "Oh, so the *women* have to stay back and pack up the cabins."

Luke smiled the charming, boyish smile that Celeste knew enabled him to get his way with most women. Even Morgan—sometimes. He kissed Morgan on the cheek. "Just two of you. The other two are coming with us. I'll let you guys decide amongst yourselves. Don't worry. Next time, we'll let you guys do the diving." He hefted the scuba gear on and headed toward the cavern, with Cal and Jake following.

Morgan turned to face her sisters. "Well, doesn't that beat all. Leaving us here. Who wants to pack, and who wants to go to the cavern?"

"You guys go. I'll stay here and pack." Celeste turned toward her cabin. Packing was probably the most useful thing she could do. At least she wouldn't have to worry about screwing that up.

"I'll stay too." Jolene got into step beside her.

"Okay, but next time, we'll do the packing," Morgan shot over her shoulder as she and Fiona jogged off toward the others.

Celeste's wet clothes from earlier were draped over the porch railing, and she pulled them off and spread them on the picnic table in the sun so they could dry before she had to pack them. Pausing, she glanced out at the ocean, picturing the pirate ships that had sailed toward here with the relic three hundred years ago. Was it really in that jeweled box? She'd been so sure when she was holding it in the cavern, but now she was nervous. What if it wasn't in there? *She'd* told them it was in the box, and if they wasted all that time only to find it was something else, it would be worse than not having found it at all. And another screw-up to add to her record.

But what difference did it make? Celeste sighed, wandering toward the cliff. Things weren't working out the way she'd hoped. Her spells had screwed everything up. She supposed the coaxing spell had led her to the store, but Jolene had already been following that trail. She'd have found the boxes with the rock in it even if Celeste weren't there, so did that even count? And, anyway, it seemed that now the rock wasn't even necessary, although it had led them to this island, so at least that was something.

Then there was the spell she'd cast to keep Dubonnet's ghost away. That had backfired and almost caused them to drown. Even the little charm that she'd cast to bring Jolene and Matteo together didn't seem to be working. She was useless.

"Glum again?" Mirabella appeared as if out of nowhere, her flowy sash fluttering in the breeze, long black hair swirling around her shoulders. Not a surprise for a ghost—they were prone to doing that.

Celeste felt a new sense of depression. Not only had she failed her sisters, she might have failed Mirabella too. If it turned out the relic had been swept away by the current, Mirabella would never get the closure she'd been waiting for all this time.

"I'm afraid I might have some bad news," Celeste said.

"About the relic hidden in Marie Antoinette's jewels?" Mirabella swirled around, brandishing her sword as if practicing fighting off an enemy.

"Yeah, well, about that relic. I had it in my hand, but I lost it."

"Lost it? How?"

Celeste sighed. "I guess it's not really lost. Not yet, anyway. The guys are diving down to try to find it."

"So you located it, then? That's half the battle."

"Yes, but it wasn't exactly where you said. I mean,

the quartz line wasn't exactly how you said it would be. But we did find the secret hiding hole in the cavern." Celeste clenched her fists. "I had that jeweled box right in my hand and let it slip away."

"Jeweled box? What are you talking about?"

Celeste's gaze flicked from the ocean to Mirabella. "The domed box with jewels on it. That's where Marie Antoinette's gems are, right?"

"No. It was never in a box. When Dubonnet was upon us, I pried the relic out of the necklace and wrapped it in part of my sash." Mirabella ran her fingers along the gold-and-magenta sash that hung at her waist. "I gave it to Constantine to hide inside the tunnels. He wanted to hide it somewhere where I could recover it should he run afoul of Dubonnet and his crew, so he told me he followed the quartz line. He etched the location on the rocks. He didn't say anything about a cavern, but we didn't have much time after that."

Wait a minute—if the relic wasn't in that box, then where was it? Maybe Cal *should* be focusing on decrypting the directions on the rocks instead of diving in the cavern. "Are you sure? The box was quite fancy. It looked like real gold and was studded with gems."

"Part of the other pirate booty that we hid. There's treasure hidden all over this island, and Marie Antoinette's jewels *were* in the domed box. But not the relic. I separated it from the others in the hopes that anyone looking for the necklace would be satisfied with what remained in the box." Mirabella frowned. "But I don't think the other treasure would not have been near the relic. Did you follow the quartz line?"

That explained why the quartz line they followed was different. It wasn't because treasure hunters had excavated different tunnels over the years—it was because they had been in the wrong place. But where was the right place? "We did follow one, but it didn't look exactly as you described."

"What about the map he etched in the rocks?"

"We're having a hard time decrypting it. Cal said it needs a columnar transposition cipher or something. Maybe you can help with that. Do you know what Constantine would have used as the cipher key?"

Mirabella shrugged. "My Constantine was very smart with those things. He was an expert navigator and could sail us to any piece of land. But me, I'm better suited to making deals and fighting. I have no head for ciphers and keys. But it must not be that hard, because the man that came before you figured it out. At least he seemed to have. I heard him say he had all the pieces."

"LeBlanc? You spoke with him? But I thought you hadn't talked to anyone but me?"

"I didn't *speak* with him. No one else has been able to see me except for you. But I can see *them*. And that man—the man that took a piece of the rock—spent many nights over the campfire, scribbling. He was alone with no one to talk to but himself. I ventured far enough to listen. He mumbled to himself that he knew where to dig and those that were after him would not find his hidden fortune. He fled in the night just as others were coming to the island. That was the last time I saw him. No one else that has come has seemed to even come close to figuring out the code."

"How do you know he didn't leave with the relic?"

"I'm still here, aren't I?" Mirabella looked at the ground, regret ghosting across her face. "Maybe if I hadn't stayed glued to this spot, I would have been able to follow him and help him out somehow. I know he was homing in on the location, but he had to leave the island quickly before he could finish. If only I'd helped him find it before he had to leave."

"But you didn't want to leave Constantine."

"Perhaps that has been my downfall. If I weren't selfishly staying here, I could have helped others not be harmed. I could have helped this LeBlanc person find the relic, but I was afraid Constantine would be lost to me forever if the relic was discovered and I wasn't near his final resting place." Mirabella bent down and placed her palm on the indentation of earth. "I also wasn't sure that LeBlanc would get the relic into the right hands. I believe he was only after the money."

"Maybe it was better you didn't help him, then," Celeste said. From what she knew, LeBlanc had no association with the people she worked for. The relic could have easily gotten into the hands of Bly's predecessor if LeBlanc had recovered it.

Mirabella looked up at Celeste. "I am sure of you, though. I know you will get it into the right hands."

"I will." Celeste felt a renewed sense of purpose. If what Mirabella was saying was true, then the box they were currently diving for in the cavern did not contain the relic.

Now she knew more than she had before. LeBlanc had decrypted the code. And if he'd been chased off the island and taken the rock to thwart the efforts of whoever was chasing him, she was sure he would have written down the cipher he used to decrypt it. And, given what Cal had explained about the columnar transposition cipher, she had a pretty good idea where he might have put it.

CHAPTER TWELVE

*C*eleste rushed back to the cabins. She had a unique opportunity to redeem herself, and she didn't want to screw that up. Inside the cabin, she rummaged in Cal's backpack for his encryption notes, which she brought back out to the picnic table. She spread all the printouts and Cal's notebooks, which included his handwritten notes, out on the table.

"What are you doing?" Jolene appeared at the doorway to her cabin, a rolled-up sleeping bag in her hand.

"The relic wasn't in that box we found."

"What? How do you know?"

Celeste tapped her finger on Cal's notebook. "I think I might know how to decrypt the code on the rocks."

Jolene frowned. "Do we need that? They're diving

for the relic right now."

Celeste shook her head. "Mirabella told me the relic wasn't in that box."

"Oh." Jolene glanced toward the cliff. "You just talked to her?"

"Yes. She said she was sure that LeBlanc had cracked the code. But when Cal looked at that section of rock over by where Bly's guys went into the tunnels, he said he thought maybe the reason he couldn't decrypt the whole thing was that he needed the key for a columnar transposition cipher."

"A what?"

"It's some kind of cipher that has letters in columns. Like rows of words."

"Okay." Jolene rummaged around in her backpack and pulled out her laptop. "So what are you thinking?"

"I think the key is in that note that LeBlanc left. The one Dorian got that started all this. It had three rows."

Celeste rummaged through the printouts they'd brought until she came to a photo of the note. "See, right here."

X MARKS the spot
   The key is hidden in plain sight
   My fortune is resolved

"LET me call up the software Cal uses to decode what's on the rocks for us." Jolene got to work on the keyboard, her fingers flying over the keys. "One problem. The three lines on the note don't have the same amount of letters, which is needed for a columnar transposition cipher."

"Maybe the empty spaces are ignored. Fill them in with nulls," Celeste suggested.

Jolene did as told, and they stared at the screen as a message formed.

Jgaroeoodfij
  Aodifgjolvf
  soreokfkdd

JOLENE SIGHED. "Well, that doesn't make much sense. Let me see if I can figure something else out." She typed some more then cursed. "Dang, that didn't work either. I'm not sure what to do. All I get is nonsensical gobbledygook. Maybe we should get Cal up here to help. He'll know what to do."

"We should, but try moving the empty spaces around. Mash the words all together, and fill the nulls in at the end." Celeste didn't want to call Cal. Not yet. Maybe she was being selfish, but she wanted a chance to prove that she could help... and if her hunch was wrong, and if by some odd chance the relic really was in that box, she didn't want to call them away from the dive and ruin their chances. Instead, she stared at Cal's decryption notes, and the clacking of the computer keys had a mesmerizing effect. Maybe the note wasn't the key. But there was something about it. The last line seemed awkward.

MY FORTUNE IS RESOLVED

THE FORTUNE!

Celeste jumped up and rushed into her cabin. Rummaging through her clothes, she tossed aside the black jeans, the gray jeans, and her yoga pants.

Jolene appeared in the doorway, a quizzical look on her face. "Now what are you doing?"

"I'm looking for the jeans I wore the day we brought those boxes back from the Chinese-food restaurant."

She spotted the faded jeans under Cal's T-shirt and grabbed them. She plunged her hand into the pocket, her fist curling around a tiny piece of paper. She pulled her hand out and held it up triumphantly. "This came out of the fortune cookie in the box. I put it in my pocket for Cal because he likes old, cryptic stuff. The cookie looked ancient."

"Okay." Jolene drew the word out.

Celeste rushed past her back to the picnic table.

"Don't you see? *My fortune is resolved.* That's what LeBlanc wrote in the note. He *did* figure out the cipher key. Resolved is another way of saying 'figured out,' right? That last line was a clue to the key." Celeste held the piece of paper up. "This is it on this little piece of paper. All those lucky letters at the bottom. He must've hidden it in the fortune cookie for some reason. Maybe someone was after him. We don't know what was going on with him. He supposedly died of a heart attack, but what if someone killed him and made it look like a heart attack?"

"A paranormal could do that. Maybe they knew he had cracked the code and killed him. But he had already put the clue in the box and hidden it in plain sight just like Dorian said," Jolene said.

"Bingo. And if that is the case, then we can use this fortune to decrypt the code."

Jolene went to the picnic table and swiveled her laptop around so they could both see the screen. Then she held her hand out for the fortune. "Let me plug this into the cipher program."

They both stared at the screen as the software worked at using the letters and numbers on the fortune to decrypt the letters on the rocks that Cal had entered earlier.

Celeste frowned as a series of letters started to

emerge. "Are you sure that's the only way to use it? Maybe we need to enter them in backwards or something."

"No, I don't think so."

"But that doesn't tell us anything. I was expecting words. You know, something like, 'take three steps north' or 'x marks the spot.'"

"Right. That's what we've been expecting, but wait..." Jolene's gaze shifted from the letters on the screen to the pictures of the rocks. "What's this here and here?" She pointed to two smaller marks.

"I thought they were some kind of separators, like punctuation or something."

"Hmm... Wait a minute. See the decrypted letters?"

"Yeah, they don't make any sense."

"Right. But notice how none of them come later in the alphabet than the letter 'I'?"

"Yeah."

Jolene pulled the computer close and copied the decrypted garbage into another program, and they both watched it spit out a series of numbers. "That's it!"

"Numbers?"

"Each letter corresponds to a number. I should have known. The etchings didn't have enough letters to contain much in the way of directions, but pirates used directions in a different way to navigate. Constantine etched in longitude and latitude. Not instructions. Coordinates."

"Really? How would he know what the longitude and latitude were three hundred years ago?"

Jolene pushed up from the table and rummaged in her backpack. "They used sextants back then. Figured it out using the stars. Longitude was easy. Latitude not so much. I'm not sure how accurate these are." Jolene glanced back at the screen. "But they are definitely coordinates. Those little marks are decimal points, and the letters at the very end actually still stand. See? So this first half is 44.5123N, which is the longitude."

"Great. Do we need a sextant to figure out where they lead?"

"Nope." Jolene held up her cell phone. "I got an app right here that will tell us. We should probably call the others..."

Celeste grabbed the phone. "We will, but first, let's see if these coordinates are even on this island. It could be a wild goose chase, and I don't want to pull them away from the dive for nothing."

"Why not? If the relic isn't in there... Hey, wait up!"

Celeste had trotted off, not wanting to wait for Jolene to call the others. A spark of hope bloomed as she navigated her way through the woods with the app. Maybe her original spell calling the clue to her hadn't failed after all. She'd been compelled to follow Jolene to the original place where they'd found the boxes, and then she'd discovered both the rock and the fortune inside the box she'd been looking in. If the fortune really had just decrypted the clue Constantine had left, giving them the coordinates, then maybe she wasn't as useless as she'd thought.

They pushed their way through branches and shrubs. Birds chirped, and squirrels scurried, going about their normal business as if unaware of the girls' important mission.

She stopped in an area that was shaded by tall pines and massive oaks and crowded with scrubby shrubs. "The good news is the coordinates are on the island. The bad news is they lead right here."

"But nothing's here." Jolene turned slowly. She was right—there were no outcroppings of rock, no caves, nothing that would gain them entrance to the tunnel system where the relic was buried.

"Maybe the latitude is off." Celeste scuffed around the forest floor, craning her neck to see if there was any kind of boulder or hill within the same longitude. She didn't see a thing—except for three gigantic tree stumps. Constantine had mentioned three large Scotch pines to Mirabella. Celeste had thought it was in relation to where he'd left the clues etched in the rock, but maybe he'd been talking about the entrance to where he'd left the relic. She started toward them.

The toe of her hiking boot hit something hard, and she stumbled.

"What's this?" She scuffed at the ground with her boot. Whatever was underfoot looked to be square.

Man-made. She bent down and brushed away the leaves and dirt to reveal a rusted square iron plate with a large, thick ring in the center. "Maybe those coordinates were right after all."

"We should call the others," Jolene said.

Celeste bent down and tugged at the ring. It barely budged. "Just help me get this open, and we'll see if anything is even under here before we bother them."

Jolene squatted down, curling her fingers around the ring. "Okay. One. Two. Three. Pull!"

Celeste pulled back as hard as she could, digging her heels into the ground and throwing her entire body weight into it. The cover lifted a hair. She gritted her teeth and pulled harder.

The cover flew open. Celeste and Jolene landed on their butts, the cover flying off to their right.

Jolene scrambled to her feet. "Looks like there *is* something here."

Celeste looked down into a dark hole. Rusted iron rungs started just under the top and continued into the darkness. She turned on Jolene's cell phone flashlight app and shined it into the hole. "It doesn't go down that far. It's only about eight feet."

She crouched down, dropping her arm into the hole to shine the light deeper. "It leads to a tunnel."

Jolene joined her at the edge of the hole, her gaze flicking from the tunnel to the western part of the island. "I think this tunnel is parallel to where Bly's guys blasted through that rock."

"Right." Celeste started down the rungs, testing them gingerly with each step to see if they would hold. The ladder creaked, but the rungs were still strong.

"Hey, wait a minute. Give me my phone back. We should call the others first. We can't just go in there," Jolene said.

Celeste hopped down to the bare dirt. A dank, wet smell came from the tunnel. She ducked inside the opening illuminating the rock walls of the tunnel with the light, the beam flashing off a thick vein of white quartz.

"This is it! We found the quartz line that Mirabella told us about."

"Great. I'll just call Luke." Jolene held her hand out for the phone, and Celeste handed it over, pulling the small flashlight out of her pocket and aiming it down the tunnel.

"They're not answering." Jolene hung up.

"Send him a text, or leave a message and let them know where we are. I'm going in. The relic could be just inside here, and we can't take the chance of Bly's guys finding it. If they came in on a parallel tunnel, they might be making their way to it right now, and I have no intention of screwing up and losing this thing a second time."

CHAPTER THIRTEEN

The dampness oozed into Celeste's bones, and the smell of dank earth permeated her nostrils as she proceeded down the tunnel, her flashlight aimed on the quartz line. She brushed a silky spiderweb from her face. Good news—apparently, no one had passed this way in a while. Or at least long enough for a spider to spin a web. From up ahead, she could hear the chirp of crickets and the light rustling of some small animal. She didn't want to think about what animal that might be.

"Hey, wait up." Jolene trotted up beside her. "I texted a message to Luke to let him know where we were. He's not going to like it."

"I know, but I just want to see if we can find the relic and then grab it and get out quickly. I don't plan to stay long, but it would take over an hour for them to stop the dive and get cleaned up then trek back up here. Bly's guys could be right behind us, and that hour could cause us to lose the relic."

She heard something back toward the entrance, like the sound of boots scraping on metal.

Jolene spun around to look behind them. "Did you hear something?"

Celeste nodded and snapped off the light. They both stood in silence, their ears straining, but no more noise came.

Celeste snapped the light on again and started forward. "Let's hurry. We may not have a lot of time."

The tunnel was wide enough for them to walk side by side, and they did, flashing their lights on the side every so often just to make sure the vein of quartz was still there. Every so often, the light would catch a spider that would quickly scurry away, the shadow from the flashlight making the insect appear much larger and almost giving Celeste heart failure.

Five minutes later, they came to a junction of three tunnels. "This is exactly as Mirabella described. I guess we take the one on the right."

Fifty feet in, a cave-like area opened up on the right side of the tunnel. It protruded out about six feet, with a low, sloping ceiling. Celeste flashed her light inside to see that the layers of rocks were shifted vertically. The quartz line they had been following veered straight up to the top of the cave. A thick spiderweb covered part of the entrance, and Celeste brushed the sticky threads away with her fingers.

"Just like Mirabella said." Jolene echoed Celeste's earlier words.

Celeste flashed her light around the bottom of the cave. While the sides were rock, the bottom was dark earth. She illuminated several spots where the dirt had been disturbed. "Looks like someone has been digging."

"Bly's men?" Jolene asked. "Do you think they've already been here and taken the relic?"

"I don't know. This doesn't look like fresh digging, and there was a web in the tunnel and on the entrance. I know spiders can spin them quickly, but no one has been here today, and if it was them, why would they fill the holes back in?" Celeste didn't want to think the relic had already been taken. This was her chance to be useful, and she hated the thought that Bly's men had beaten her to it.

"Right. We should still look, but where *exactly* is it? Did Mirabella give you any clues?"

"She just said where the line shoots straight up." Celeste pointed at Jolene's phone. "What about the coordinates?"

Jolene looked down at the phone. "They only led to where we found the entrance. They aren't that precise, and they couldn't judge latitude accurately back in

Constantine's day. I'm afraid this is as close as we can get."

"Then it could be anywhere." Celeste looked around the cave.

"Yeah, but the quartz vein is in here, and it goes straight up, so I say we start here." Jolene crouched directly under the spot where the quartz line veered upward. She pulled the pickax out of her belt. "Good thing I brought this." She plunged the sharp end into the dirt then used the side to scrape it away.

"Maybe we should've brought Fiona. She might have been able to ferret it out by using her special gifts." Celeste hadn't brought any kind of digging tool, so she poked her fingers into one of the already dug-up holes and scooped out a handful of dirt. A cool breeze raised goose bumps on her arm. Celeste jerked her attention toward the cave opening. Was something swirling out there? A ghost? "What was that? Do you feel a breeze?" she asked.

"No." Jolene squinted into the darkness behind Celeste. "I don't see any energy trails or anything, but then again, ghosts don't usually leave them. If Dubonnet is behind us, then I guess you'll have to keep an eye out. I won't be able to see him."

"Right. What can he do, anyway? We're not afraid of him unless he's able to move physical objects." Celeste paused. Normally, ghosts couldn't interact with physical objects. Sure, they could push something off a table once in a while or mess with electricity if they concentrated really hard, but they didn't usually even do those things. It took a lot of energy, and in her experience, ghosts were mostly lazy. But hadn't Fiona said something about the energy of certain rocks being able to give ghosts different powers over the physical realm? Celeste glanced uneasily at the granite rock on the sides and ceiling of the tunnel. Was granite one of those rocks?

"What's that?" Jolene had stopped digging. A frown creased her face as she gazed out of the cave toward the tunnel they'd come in through.

Celeste stilled to listen. Was that some sort of scratching sound? "I heard something, too. Maybe we should go back and—"

"*Meow.*"

"Belladonna!" The tension eased out of Celeste's shoulders as the cat trotted over to sniff at the hole where she was digging. "I should have known she would have followed us."

"Yeah. Now if she could just help us dig," Jolene said.

As if understanding Jolene's words, Belladonna lazily walked to a spot just under the quartz vein and started digging.

"I knew you were a smart kitty." Celeste scratched the cat behind the ears as Belladonna's front paws worked to soften the earth. Brown chunks of dirt spewed out, the smell of fresh earth wafting up. Dirt, small rocks, a seashell—and then her heart skipped when she caught a glimpse of magenta and gold.

"Stop!"

Belladonna stopped, sat back on her haunches, licked one paw, and blinked at Celeste lazily.

Celeste brushed her fingers across the silky fabric. It was frayed and worn, but there was no mistaking what it was. Mirabella's sash. She poked her fingers gently into the hole, wedging the sash and its contents out.

"What is it?" Jolene asked.

"If I'm not mistaken, this is Mirabella's sash. The one she hid the gem in." Celeste carefully unwrapped the sash to reveal a large oval stone. The sash had kept it from getting dirty, and it blinked up at them with rainbow luminescence.

"That's it!" Jolene stared at the gem. "I recognize it from the picture online. You found the relic."

Celeste's heart swelled with pride. She really had found it. She *was* useful after all. "Let's get it out of here quickly before Bly's guys get here."

Celeste carefully wrapped the relic back up in the sash, and the girls stood. When she turned toward the cave exit, Celeste's heart jerked in her chest. A dark figure barred their exit.

"Thanks for doing all the dirty work for me. Now hand over the treasure."

CHAPTER FOURTEEN

*T*he ghost was dressed in swashbuckler clothing. He had a long beard and was wearing a flowing white shirt and held a giant sword that gleamed in the light as he waved it in the air. He pointed the sword toward Celeste and raised a bushy black brow.

"Dubonnet?" Celeste asked.

"Aye. Now hand over the gem, or I'll cut you to pieces."

"Is that Mirabella's enemy?" Jolene asked.

Celeste moved between her sister and Dubonnet. Jolene couldn't see ghosts, which made her vulnerable. She wouldn't be able to avoid him if he came at her, and while ghosts couldn't do much harm unless they managed to envelop a human entirely in their misty aura, Celeste didn't want to take any chances. "Yes, it is."

"Really? Then why can I see him?"

Celeste flashed a look over her shoulder at Jolene. "You can *see* him?"

Her eyes fell on the quartz line. It was as she'd feared. The proximity of the rocks and the centuries he'd been down here had given Dubonnet the powers of manifesting in the physical realm, just as Fiona had said. That was why Jolene could see him, and unfortunately, that meant the menacing sword he was waving around could actually hurt them.

"He's manifested in the physical realm because of the rocks," Celeste said.

"Never mind that." Dubonnet took a step closer, thrusting out his hand. The hairs on the back of Celeste's neck stood on end. Something was vaguely familiar about the pirate. "Hand it over."

Celeste clenched the relic tighter in her fist. She tensed her body for a karate kick, her only means of defense. She didn't know how good the ghost's reflexes were, but if she lashed out at him and he was quick, that sword could do some real damage. Would a karate kick even damage him, though? Her leg would normally pass through most ghosts, but Dubonnet seemed almost solid. He wasn't swirling with mist like all the others she'd encountered. If the effects of the energy from the rocks made him able to manifest in the physical realm, then it stood to reason that he could be felled by a well-placed karate kick the same as a human.

She glanced at Jolene, who was rubbing her palms together, getting ready to hit Dubonnet with some energy. "I don't know if that's such a good idea," Celeste said out of the corner of her mouth. "If he's a ghost, he's probably amped up with energy. I don't know what will happen if you hit him with more."

"Well, what else can we do?" Jolene asked as they backed into the cave and farther away from Dubonnet, who was advancing on them.

"Never mind that. I've got you cornered, so just hand it over, and no one will get hurt," Dubonnet said.

Jolene snorted. "Right. Like you didn't hurt that guy up in the treasure pit who succumbed to the gas."

Dubonnet's eyes narrowed, and he stepped closer. "No one can steal my treasure. Have you not heard the rumors? Many have tried, and many have died. The treasure in these tunnels is mine."

"So you *are* behind all those deaths of treasure hunters that came to the island?" Celeste wanted to keep him talking, buying time until she could figure out how to overpower him.

"Aye. They were trespassers and thieves."

"I think *you* are the thief. You stole the treasure from Mirabella." Jolene kept rubbing her hands together, and Celeste could see the purple glow of energy building in between her cupped palms, the light shining out between her fingers.

"'Tis the way of pirates. I won fair and square. Now just hand that treasure over, and be gone. I will let you run as I have let others run." Dubonnet waved the sword again.

"You let others go?" Celeste asked.

"Yes. If not, then no one would be left to tell the tales. To warn the others away."

"Seems like that worked, but what in the world are you going to do with treasure anyway?" Jolene asked.

"That's none of your concern." Dubonnet lurched forward, waving the shiny sword near Jolene's face. "Now tell your sister to hand it over, or your fate will be unpleasant indeed."

"*Meow.*"

All heads jerked toward Belladonna.

"Go home, Belladonna. You don't want to get hurt." Celeste's stomach twisted. That sword could do some real damage to Belladonna, and the cat was known for putting herself in harm's way. But would Dubonnet hurt an innocent cat?

Thankfully, the ghost wasn't paying any attention to Belladonna. His gaze was fixed on the relic as he slowly backed them up against the far end of the cave. Celeste shifted to the left, trying to force their movements so that he wouldn't be blocking the exit. But even if she could manipulate it so that she could get out past him, could she outrun him?

Maybe his powers didn't work outside the tunnels. That was probably why he'd stayed down here. Fiona had said his superpowers of manifesting in the physical realm had something to do with the energy from the rocks that surrounded them in the tunnel, so it was a good bet he would lose that ability outside. But ghosts were fast. She doubted she could outrun him, but maybe if she could distract him, Jolene could make a run for safety.

"I know what you're thinking. Don't even try it," he said. "I'm faster than you think." He jabbed the sword at her, catching the edge of her hoodie and slicing a tear in it. Yep, that thing was real, *and* it was sharp.

"Okay, that's it!" Jolene flung out her fist, and a stream of purple energy sparked from it, hitting the sides of the cave and ricocheting around. They ducked the ping-ponging stream, Dubonnet's eyes growing wide as the energy fizzled out and dissipated into the ground.

"What the heck—"

"*Meow!*"

Belladonna launched herself at Dubonnet. Her claws caught on his beard, the weight of the cat pulling it away from his face. The fake beard fell to the ground, and Celeste's eyes widened at what was underneath.

"Jason?"

* * *

CELESTE COULDN'T BELIEVE IT. It wasn't Dubonnet's ghost standing in front of them—it was Jason, the man who had driven them to the island in his boat.

"Yes, it's me. I'm not a ghost. The ghost disguise usually works pretty well to scare people off. I figured you people would be trouble, but I wanted to get the treasure the easy way." He glared down at Belladonna, who was standing at Celeste's feet, her back arched and fur on end. "Now it looks like things might have to get messy."

"But how did you know we were here in this tunnel?" Now that she knew their attacker was a mere human, Celeste felt a little better about her ability to help defend them. She saw Jolene inching toward the cave exit and readied herself, tensing her muscles to do battle with Jason. A few well-placed kicks could easily disable him, and unless he was a black belt himself, she had a good chance of succeeding. Hopefully, she'd be able to avoid the menacing sword he still held in his hand.

"I didn't. Not exactly. But when Luke called for me to come pick you up from the island, I figured that meant you'd found something." He looked around the cavern. "All my years of research have indicated there's treasure in this cavern."

"So you've been coming to the island looking for treasure for years?" Celeste asked.

"Yep. Luckily, no one comes here anymore. Too many rumors of it being haunted and booby-trapped. So I get to take my time and come when I can. Usually."

"You mean you killed people and arranged accidents to get others to stay away?" Jolene asked.

Jason's jaw twitched. "I never killed anyone. That was before my time. But I took advantage of the old legends to help dissuade people from coming. And those that did... well... I did what I had to do to scare them off."

"So you could have the treasure for yourself," Celeste said. "But you didn't scare us off because we were simply doing a documentary."

Jason scoffed. "You guys don't think I fell for that made-up story about you being out here to do a documentary, do you? I planned to scare you off but couldn't come out sooner. Christian was ill. I knew you were coming for treasure, just like Stanford McMillan."

"Stanford McMillan?"

"The last guy that came here a few years ago."

Celeste had been under the impression no one had been to the island seeking treasure in decades. Jason snorted at the quizzical look the girls exchanged. "Yeah, you probably didn't hear about him in the news or find out about him in your research, right? That's

because plenty of people come here looking for treasure, and they don't exactly announce it. You wouldn't
believe how many people have been here digging
around. I usually end up being able to scare them off
pretty quickly, but Stanford was persistent."

"And you and all these other people have been
digging in the tunnels all these years and never found
any treasure?"

"I never said *no one* found treasure." Anger flashed
in Jason's eyes. "But I found out long ago that when it
comes to treasure, it's every man for himself. And I'm
not going to let you take advantage of all my hard
work." He gestured toward all the dig marks in the
ground. "I've been digging here for treasure for years. I
need it more than anyone."

Jason's face softened, and Celeste's heart melted as
the look of anger in his eyes turned to sadness. That
desperate look told her he wasn't seeking the treasure
for greed or monetary gain. He needed it for his son's
medical treatment.

Then his face turned dark again, and he lunged for
the relic.

Celeste sidestepped then blocked him with a karate
kick to the forearm.

"Ouch!" Jason whirled around, landing his own
kick and dislodging the relic from Celeste's grasp. It
landed upside down in the dirt, but Celeste didn't have
a chance to retrieve it before Jason kicked again. Out of

the corner of her eye, she saw Jolene gearing up for another energy blast.

"Wait!" she yelled to Jolene as she rolled on the floor with Jason, trying to pin him down. She didn't want Jolene to hurt him. He was only trying to help his kid, and she knew a way they could both get what they wanted.

Celeste broke free and sprang to her feet. Jason was on his feet just as quickly.

Celeste held her hand up. "Wait. We can help you."

Jason snorted. "That's what Stanley said. Said we'd split the treasure. I led him to all the spots I'd researched. Then he dug up a cache of gold coins and took off, leaving me with nothing but a child that was getting weaker and weaker."

"But we're not after the treasure like you think. Not for money. We're only after this one gem." Celeste pointed to the relic still lying in the dirt. "This is an old energy-infused relic. It has special properties. It can ward off negative energy. But that's of no use to most people, and we can get you more money than what you could sell this gem for. We can help your son get the treatment he needs."

"You think I'm going to fall for some stupid story about an energy-infused gemstone? Why should I trust you? I trusted Stanley, and he screwed me over. You'll probably do it too."

"No, we won't. I swear." Jolene inched toward the

relic. She sidestepped toward it, bending her knees and leaning down.

Jason crouched too, holding the sword high. Celeste could see he was poised to lunge after Jolene. She didn't know what he planned to do with the sword, but she did know that he'd have a hard time wielding the weapon and grabbing the relic at the same time.

Celeste readied herself to tackle Jason. As soon as Jolene had the relic in her hand, she would shout for her to run, tackle Jason, and hopefully put him out of commission while Jolene got away with the relic.

"Grab that gem, and I'll have to take it by force. You'll never—"

The heavy thudding of boots running down the tunnel toward them stopped him midsentence.

They turned to see two bearded guys standing in the entrance, waving bazooka-like energy guns even larger than the one Buzz had found earlier. Bly's guys.

"Hand over the relic, or we'll turn you all to ashes."

CHAPTER FIFTEEN

*T*he two men blocked the exit. One of them was tall and lanky, the other a little shorter but broader in the shoulders. Both of them had big guns pointed menacingly at Celeste, Jolene, and Jason. Celeste noticed the shorter one had a bandana wrapped around his hand. He must have been the one that had been holding the gun Buzz found, and sustained the injury when the rocks fused together, leaving the gun on the outside. If she had to fight them, she'd aim for that hand. An injury was always a weak spot. Why hadn't they taken the time to figure out how to work that gun? Maybe they could have used it to fight these guys.

Jolene jumped in front of Celeste. "You guys know you're no match for me."

The tall one's bushy left eyebrow quirked up. "Seriously? We have these big guns. They shoot negative energy. *Deadly* negative energy. Just hand it over, and no one will get hurt." His eyes narrowed as they shifted from Jolene to Celeste and then to Jason. Apparently, he was trying to figure out which one of them had the relic, not realizing it was lying in the dirt right behind them.

"Right. I wasn't born yesterday. You're not getting the relic without a fight." Jolene shifted subtly so that she was in front of the relic, blocking them from seeing it on the ground.

The tall thug shrugged. "Have it your way."

He aimed his gun at Jolene while at the same time she thrust her palms out toward him. A dark-brown stream of energy flew from his gun. A light-purple stream of light flew from Jolene's hand. The energy streams met in the middle in a blinding flash and...

Kaboom!

The ground shook, and rocks rained down from the top of the cavern. Celeste's heart knocked against her rib cage as she fought to stay upright despite the shaking ground. Would the whole tunnel cave in?

The shaking stopped, and everyone scurried to regain their balance.

Celeste glanced nervously at Belladonna, trying to telepath for the cat to take her chance to escape. The men didn't seem to be paying any attention to her, and she didn't want her to get hurt. Knowing the cat, she might jump up and try to claw one of the men, and Celeste shuddered to think what would happen to Belladonna if they turned their energy guns on her. Too bad the cat couldn't read minds. She could pick the relic up in her mouth and trot off. But Belladonna sat tight, watching the five of them with anxious blue eyes.

Jason hung back behind them and off to the side as the two men advanced, backing them against the wall of the cavern.

Jolene rubbed her hands together, a move that told Celeste she was summoning more fighting energy. "Better be careful in here. The energy ricochets off the rocks. You could end up hitting yourself. Maybe we can settle this without shooting a lot of energy around."

"Sure. Hand over the relic, and it will be settled," the shorter one said.

"That's not exactly what I had in mind." What *did* Jolene have in mind? Celeste figured she must be stalling, giving herself time to build up more energy. Too bad Celeste couldn't help with that. The only thing she could do was use her karate skills to try to disarm one of the men. She tensed her muscles, ready to kick out if she saw the chance.

"I don't see you have much choice here. Looks like your energy is not up to par. I don't think it's any match for our weapons." The tall one shot a look at Jason.

"Unless maybe your pirate friend here is going to make us walk the plank."

The two men burst out laughing.

The distraction was Celeste's chance! She kicked out toward the shorter one, aiming for the bandana-wrapped hand. His reflexes were quick. He spun and aimed his gun at her. His quick movement caused her foot to miss him, and she fell off balance as he shot directly at her.

She managed to grab her obsidian talisman just in the nick of time, shoving it in the way of the ugly negative-energy stream. The stream hit her talisman, heating it to scorching temperatures, then bounced off and headed toward the side of the cavern. A puff of smoke appeared as it drilled a small hole into the white quartz vein in the wall.

The tall guy wasted no time aiming his gun at Jolene, who was caught between sending more energy out and using her talisman to deflect the energy coming toward her. She opted for the talisman. The negative energy hit it and exploded into a million brown sparks that fell to the ground, twinkling like malevolent fireflies.

Celeste caught a movement behind the men. In the fighting, Jason had slipped behind them and was running down the tunnel. Her eyes jerked to the spot where the relic had fallen. It wasn't there.

Jason had run off with the relic.

In a blur of white fur, Belladonna took off after him. Celeste felt a small measure of relief. At least the cat wouldn't get hurt by any stray energy bouncing around.

"Hey, he took the relic!" Celeste pointed to the tunnel.

The tall guy smirked. "Right. We're not going off on a wild goose chase. You guys would lie to protect it, and the boss said you *girls* would have it. He won't have time to gather reinforcements. We're ending this here and now."

He shot again. Celeste held out the amulet, but its powers were growing weaker. It had absorbed too much energy already. Some of the energy oozed out and hit her shoulder. She lost the feeling in her arm. It fell limply to her side, the amulet dropping against her chest.

"Leave her alone!" Jolene threw a ball of red flaming energy at the tall guy and stepped in front of Celeste.

He dodged the energy ball, and it smacked against the wall of the tunnel, fell to the ground, and then rolled out of sight.

He aimed his gun at Jolene. She whipped out her pendant just as he shot, but like Celeste, it seemed that the stone's ability to absorb energy was weakening. Only part of the energy was absorbed. The rest streamed over her, and she fell to the ground.

Celeste crouched next to her, taking her hand. "We'll be more powerful together."

The tall man laughed. "I see your amulets are doing you no good. You are both weak now and are no match for me. Hand over the relic now, and I might let you live."

"I told you. We don't have it." Jolene flung her fingers out, and sparks of white-hot energy peppered the men, singeing their thick camouflage jackets.

They beat at their jackets with their hands, cursing Jolene and Celeste. Jolene tried frantically to raise more energy while they were distracted. Celeste shook her arm, regaining a little movement but not enough to be useful. She gripped Jolene's fingers tight with her good hand and willed her extra energy into her sister.

Unfortunately, the energy sparks had only served to drain Jolene further while increasing the thugs' anger. They both raised their guns, leveling them at the two girls. Brown energy shot toward them.

Celeste dropped Jolene's hand and grabbed her amulet, holding it toward the stream. Jolene shoved hers out next to Celeste's, the sides of the stones touching. Maybe the two amulets together would have increased power.

But they didn't. Paralyzing energy coursed through Celeste, zapping her like a high-voltage wire. She fell back on the ground, her breath coming in sharp rasps.

Jolene lay next to her, her face twisted in pain, her body twitching.

"I'll give you one last chance to produce the relic and hand it over nicely before we finish you off and take the relic from your dead bodies." The short man aimed again.

"For the last time, we don't have it. The pirate took it."

The men exchanged a look.

"I don't think we should believe them," the tall guy said.

"What difference does it make? We should finish them off and search the bodies, and if they don't have the relic, we'll go after the pirate."

"Good idea." They raised their guns and fired.

Celeste screwed her eyes shut, holding her breath against the pain of the jolt of energy that would kill her.

CHAPTER SIXTEEN

eleste waited for the painful energy zap, but instead she heard a scuffle and then, "No, you don't!"

Her eyes flew open to see Jason standing in between her and the bad guys. He was holding the relic up like a shield as if to protect them from the bad-energy guns.

"So the pirate really did have the relic. How convenient of you to bring it to us." The tall guy smirked at Jason. "I hope you don't think that little thing is going to keep us from shooting you."

Celeste struggled to her feet. Jason glanced over his shoulder at her and Jolene. "Are you guys okay?"

"They might be okay now, but in a few seconds, the three of you will be dead," the short guy cut in. "Unless you want to just hand it over. Then we'll let you go. The other two, I'm not sure about."

Jason shook his head. "No way. I know what happens when you trust someone. You'll take the jewel, but you won't let me go."

"Okay, then. Have it your way." The short guy aimed right at Jason. "Full force!"

The men flicked a lever on their guns and then aimed and shot. Thick black tar-like jets of energy hurtled out of the guns, forming one big river of dark energy headed straight toward them. Jason stepped right in front of it, shoving the relic into the vile stream.

The energy hit the relic with a sharp crack.

A wet slapping sound filled the air. The tang of ozone stung Celeste's nostrils.

The energy boomeranged straight back toward the two thugs.

The two thugs were covered in the black tar-like goo. A jolt of electricity illuminated their skeletons like an x-ray. A bright-blue flash followed, and the men turned a chalky shade of gray. They stood stock still, their faces frozen with shocked expressions of disbelief, and then they dissolved into fine gray ash that floated to the floor in two distinct piles.

"Holy heck." Jason stared at the piles.

"You can say that again." Jolene struggled to her feet.

"Wow, I guess that thing really is a super energy deflector." Celeste pushed up from the floor and looked over Jason's shoulder at the now-blackened gem still nestled inside Mirabella's sash. "But why did you come back?"

"That cat kept getting in my way. Running in front of me in the tunnel. She tripped me a few times. Stopped me from leaving. Because of her, I didn't make it very far down the tunnel and could hear you fighting with those guys." Jason glanced uneasily at the piles of ashes. "I'm not sure what the heck is going on here with those weird guns and the... energy. I'd seen you using your amulets and thought you would be okay, but then when I was in the tunnel, it sounded like you were losing. I couldn't just leave and let you get hurt. Then I remembered what you said about the gem being some sort of super energy absorber, and I took a chance and ran back."

"Well, thanks. We're glad you did," Celeste said.

"*Meow!*" Belladonna trotted into the center of their circle, flicking her tail.

Jolene bent down and scratched the cat between the ears. "You too, Belladonna."

"Yeah, well." Jason drew in a breath and looked down at the gem, which now resembled a worthless piece of coal. "Too bad I ruined the treasure. This is worth nothing now. I may have saved you, but in doing so, I may also have ruined things for my son."

"I don't think it's ruined." Jolene held her hand out for the relic, and Jason placed it in her palm. She wrapped the sash around it then cupped her other palm over it and closed her eyes. After a few seconds, she pulled her top hand away and pushed the sash aside. One tiny spot in the very center of the stone glowed with a faint pulse of rainbow-colored light for a second. "I think it just absorbed so much energy that it needs to be revitalized."

"*Meow.*" Belladonna rubbed her cheek against Jason's calf, and he bent down to pet her. "That's great, but it still doesn't help my boy."

Celeste put an arm around him and started toward the exit. "Let's get out of here and back to the camp. We need to call the others, but I don't want you to worry about your boy. We really can help. In fact, I think our friends over at the cavern are digging up something that can help you right now."

Hope sparked on Jason's face. "Really? Why would you guys help me?"

"We've been blessed with plenty for ourselves, and we like to give back. Right, Jolene?"

Jolene nodded. "Yep, we have more than enough for us."

Jason hesitated, looking from Celeste to Jolene. "Wow, I don't know what to say."

"You don't have to say a thing," Jolene said.

"But I've got plenty to say," a voice boomed behind

them, and Celeste spun around to see a swirly mist solidifying into the large mass of a pirate. *This* time, Celeste knew she really was seeing a ghost.

Dubonnet was standing in the tunnel, brandishing a sword, and he did not look happy.

CHAPTER SEVENTEEN

"*D*ubonnet," Celeste said.
"One and the same."

"But that can't be. Am I seriously seeing a ghost?" Jason stared at the swirly apparition. "Then again, this might not be the strangest thing I've seen today."

"That's right!" The ghost brandished a long sword, swirling the carved-steel blade in the air and then poking it out toward Celeste, who jumped back instinctively. "This has been my domain for centuries. I've made sure no one steals my treasures. I laid claim to this island long ago, and any treasure you've found in these tunnels is mine. So hand it over."

"I don't think so, Dubonnet. This treasure belongs to Mirabella de Lafleur. You slaughtered Mirabella and her crew to steal her treasure."

"Aye. That's why I'm the better pirate. To the

winner go the spoils!" Dubonnet laughed, an evil sound that echoed through the tunnels. He spun around, slashing his sword against the side of the tunnel with a metallic clang. Sparks flew where metal met rock. He spun back around and stepped closer to Celeste, Jason, and Jolene. "As you see, my threat is real. I've made mincemeat of many and will do the same to you."

"We're not handing it over," Jolene said.

Dubonnet stilled, his eyes narrowed on Jolene. "No? You are foolish. How would you fight me? You don't even have weapons."

Jolene flexed the hand that wasn't holding the relic. "We have our ways."

Celeste bit her bottom lip. Clearly, Jolene was planning to zap Dubonnet with some energy, but Celeste had no idea what would happen if she did. Ghosts were a different type of energy themselves, and she doubted the results would be the same as when they battled people. Then again, it didn't look as though they had much choice.

"*Meow!*" Belladonna launched herself at Dubonnet. The attack must have taken him by surprise. He shrank back from the cat, his swirly mist breaking up where the cat sailed through him and landed behind him.

"Contain that beast!" He swiped the sword toward Belladonna, who leaped away. Her body twisted in the air, but she landed on all fours.

"Belladonna, look out!" Jolene shoved the relic into Celeste's hands and unfurled her fist, sending blue energy toward Dubonnet's sword.

The energy hit the tip of the sword, swathing it in blue light that ran up the length to Dubonnet's hand.

"Arghh!" He cradled his hand but did not drop the sword. His body turned translucent for a second, as if he might evaporate, but then he steeled himself and turned even more solid, almost as if becoming flesh and blood.

He turned his fury on the three of them. "Now I will show no mercy!"

He slashed out toward Jason, catching him in the leg.

"Ack!" Jason fell to the ground, a slash of blood welling down the side of his calf where the blade had struck.

Dubonnet spun around, hitting Jolene in the hand, causing the energy ball she was working on to fall to the floor and roll down the tunnel. He kicked out at her ankles, and she fell with a thud.

Celeste leapt toward him, unfurling her leg in a kick aimed at his sword hand. But Dubonnet was neither flesh and blood nor ectoplasmic mist. He was something in between, and her foot connected with a slimy, soft substance, which threw her off balance. She landed flat on her back next to Jolene and Jason.

Dubonnet laughed, his body looming over them.

He raised his sword high in the air. "No one steals my treasure!"

He let out a yell, and his sword plunged downward.

"Not so fast, Dubonnet!" A voice rang out from the tunnel behind the ghost.

Dubonnet fumbled, whirling around before the razor-sharp sword could strike them.

Celeste squinted through Dubonnet's swirling form to see Mirabella standing behind him, her gleaming sword held in a fighting stance in front of her.

"You! I thought I took care of you centuries ago." Dubonnet swished his sword through the air.

"Looks like we get another chance to fight." Mirabella circled to the left, Dubonnet to the right, the two ghosts keeping two feet of space between them.

"You won't win this time either," Dubonnet sneered then leapt forward, jabbing out at Mirabella.

Mirabella lunged back then spun around, her sword slicing through the air at waist height.

Dubonnet slashed his sword down at an angle. Mirabella met his thrust, her sword clanking against his sword.

Mirabella slashed right. Dubonnet blocked it with his sword and spun left.

Sparks flew, and the tunnel was filled with the sound of metal clashing with metal as the two ghosts battled it out.

"Quick! We must do something to help her!" Jolene rubbed her hands together, producing a ball of blue energy that glowed in between her palms.

Celeste held out her arm to stop her sister. "Not yet. I think Mirabella needs to do this on her own."

Dubonnet jabbed at Mirabella.

Mirabella lurched back. She raised her sword high over her head then lunged at Dubonnet, bringing the sword straight down and slicing it directly through the middle of his ghostly body. The metal blade of the sword glowed bright red as it cleaved through the ectoplasmic energy that made up Dubonnet's ghostly form.

Two piles of misty goo fell to the floor.

Celeste held her breath. Would the two piles rise up and reconnect to form Dubonnet's ghost, or was he gone for good? She had no idea of how to get rid of a ghost or how the effects of the energy from the rock tunnel would affect it, but she did know that separating the ectoplasm that made up his body as a whole might be enough to send him on to the next plane, whatever that might be.

As they watched, the piles melted to water and drained into the ground.

Dubonnet was gone.

Mirabella shoved her sword back into the scabbard on her waist. "I've been waiting three hundred years to do that."

She turned to them, her eyes falling on the

magenta-and-gold sash that Jolene held in her hand. "You found the relic."

"We did." Jolene opened her fist to show the relic nestled in the fabric.

Mirabella frowned. "It doesn't look quite the same as it did when I put it in there."

"Yeah, we kind of had to use it to defend ourselves. Don't worry—it will be restored to its former potential." Jolene looked Mirabella up and down. "This is cool. I've never been able to see ghosts before."

"It's the energy from the rocks that surround us." Celeste pointed to the granite tunnel.

Mirabella nodded and clapped a ghostly hand on Celeste's shoulder, causing a frigid sensation to drill directly into Celeste's arm. Inside the tunnel, ghosts were a lot more solid. Normally, a ghost's hand would pass right through her. Celeste shivered, and Mirabella pulled away.

"Good job. Now we must get this into the rightful hands before someone else comes and takes it away," Mirabella said.

As they started toward the exit, Celeste sensed sadness in Mirabella's demeanor despite her victory over Dubonnet.

"Why did you leave the cliff? You've risked your future with Constantine," Celeste said. A few feet ahead, a round patch of light splayed on the tunnel floor, indicating the entrance.

Mirabella pursed her lips together. "I saw this one come in his boat and head toward the tunnel." She pointed to Jason. "I know why he comes, and I know he is no threat, but I kept watch. Then, from my vantage point on the cliff, I saw Dubonnet swirling around the underwater caves near the cove. I knew you were close to recovering the relic and he would come after you. *This time*, I couldn't sit back and let him do harm."

"Even if it meant you wouldn't be with Constantine on the other side?" They were at the entrance now, and Celeste glanced up just to make sure Bly hadn't sent reinforcements who might be waiting outside. The coast appeared to be clear, so she grasped a rung of the gritty rusted metal ladder and started to climb.

Mirabella was right behind her. "It was the right thing to do. I regretted not stepping in before. Maybe Karma will see that Constantine and I are together."

They reached the top, and Mirabella swirled uncertainly, nodding at Celeste. "Our journey is done. Thank you for recovering the relic. I thought once my mission was accomplished, I would be able to move on, but I don't feel any different. Perhaps my fate is to stay on this island alone after all."

Mirabella's body was more transparent than normal. Something was happening. "No, I think something is different. You seem more faded. You might be going home now."

"Faded?" Jolene climbed up out of the hole. "I can't see her at all."

"That's because we're out of the tunnel and the effects of the rock energy that allow her to manifest physically are gone." Celeste turned to Mirabella. "Maybe you should hurry back to the cliff. It may not be too late to catch Constantine."

Mirabella gave a curt nod and rushed off in the direction of the cliff. Coming over the horizon was another ghost. A tall, handsome pirate.

"Constantine!" Mirabella rushed to the ghost with open arms. He whirled her around. Mirabella's laugh and the wide smiles on their faces warmed Celeste's heart. They were fading together, and she could barely make out Mirabella turning to her with a wave.

Celeste felt more than heard Mirabella's words. "Thank you."

And then they were gone.

"What happened?" Jolene was squinting in the direction of the ghosts.

"I think things are going to work out okay for Mirabella and Constantine." Celeste turned toward Jolene. Over her shoulder, Celeste saw Matteo rushing toward them, his eyes full of concern for Jolene.

A rush of optimism ran through Celeste. Her spells weren't such a failure after all. She'd found the relic and managed to save it from Bly's guys. She'd contributed to the mission instead of being just a useless tag-along, and as a bonus, she was going to be able to help Jason's son get the treatment he needed. And, if her spells really did work, then maybe the charm she'd laid for Matteo and Jolene would help bring them together.

Matteo rushed to Jolene, pulling her to him. She didn't resist. Celeste thought maybe she saw a secret smile on her sister's face as she let Matteo hug her.

Celeste glanced down at the relic then nodded at Jason and then Jolene. "In fact, I think things are going to work out okay all around."

CHAPTER EIGHTEEN

*L*uke, Cal, Jake, Gordy, Buzz, Morgan, and Fiona showed up right behind Matteo. Cal rushed over to Celeste, slipping his arm around her.

"Are you guys okay? We got your text. Did you go in yet?" Luke asked.

Jolene stuck out her hand, showing them the relic, which was still nestled in the sash in the middle of her palm.

"Is that it?" Fiona ran her palm over the stone. It pulsed faintly with blue, purple, and red.

"Yep. We've got it."

Luke ran his fingers through his short-cropped hair. "It's great you retrieved it, but you guys shouldn't have gone in there alone with Bly's guys hanging around. That was risky."

Jolene winked at Celeste. "We can take care of ourselves."

"Yeah, but still, you should have waited for us." Morgan turned a skeptical eye on Jason. "What's with the getup?"

Jason's shoulders slumped, and he looked down at the ground.

Celeste cut in before he could say anything. "Jason was playing with Christian when he got your message calling him to the island. He rushed right over for us without even changing. Good thing too, because he helped us fight off Bly's thugs."

"*Meow.*" Belladonna sat in the sun, twitching her tail and glaring at Celeste.

"Oh, and Belladonna helped too," Celeste added.

"Wait a minute. You fought Bly's men in there? By yourselves?" Fiona's eyes darkened with concern, and she turned to Jolene. "You know you're not supposed to rush off and do things alone, especially if you might run into enemy paranormals. The four of us are stronger together."

"It wasn't Jolene's fault. It was my fault," Celeste said. "I saw Mirabella when we were packing up, and she gave me a hint that allowed me to decrypt the code."

"You decrypted it?" Cal looked at her with a mixture of pride and curiosity.

"Yes. But we didn't want to call you guys up from

the dive in the cavern on a wild goose chase, so we figured we'd just take a quick look to see if we were on the right trail," Celeste said.

"But then Bly's guys must've been watching, or maybe they were coming here anyway. They cornered us," Jolene added.

"We fought them but wouldn't have won without Jason," Celeste said. "Bly's guys had strong negative-energy guns. Our amulets had absorbed the maximum amount of energy and were wearing out. We were almost done for when Jason selflessly jumped into the negative-energy stream with the relic. The relic boomeranged that energy back to Bly's thugs."

Morgan looked uncertainly at the entrance hole. "And where are they now?"

"They're in there. Two piles of ash. I guess that relic really is powerful," Jolene said. "And then we had some ghostly intervention."

"You did? That ghost pirate that's rumored to haunt the tunnels? Did he attack?" Fiona asked.

"Yes, and Mirabella rushed in to save the day. That ended in our favor too," Celeste said.

"You guys were lucky, but I don't want you to do that again. I guess it's over with now, and we should focus on getting out of here and get that relic to Dorian as soon as we can." Luke started walking back toward the cabins, and they all followed.

Cal clapped Jason on the back. "Thanks for helping out in there."

"Yeah." Jake shook Jason's hand. "But how did you know to use the relic against the energy streams?"

"We told him about it. When he came upon us in the cavern and saw us with it, we explained why it was important," Celeste said. "Which reminds me, Jason saved our lives, and now we owe him. You know how we always repay our debts."

"Ummm, yeah..." Morgan slid a glance at Celeste out of the corner of her eye.

"Jason needs money for medical treatment for Christian," Celeste said.

Morgan nodded. "We have plenty of that, but it's all tied up in trusts and investments."

Celeste nodded. She knew it would take a long time to free up their money, but she had a better idea. "How did the dive go? Did you find that box?"

"We did," Morgan said. "But, as you know, the relic wasn't in there."

"What *was* in there?" Jolene asked.

"Some gold escudos, Spanish cobs, and an old gold cross," Fiona said as they spilled out into the clearing where the cabins were. She pointed to the picnic table, where the domed box sat in plain view. "Check it out for yourself."

Celeste stared at Fiona incredulously. "You left it right out on the table where anyone could get it?"

Fiona shrugged. "Since it wasn't critical to our mission, we didn't consider it very important, and we were in kind of a hurry after getting your text. Hiding it might have wasted valuable time. The last we heard was you were going into the tunnel, and we received no further texts, so we didn't know if you had met with trouble inside the tunnel."

Celeste flipped open the box. Inside was a cache of gold coins in two sizes, their edges clipped and uneven but the gold still brilliant in color. She picked up one of the larger ones—an 8 escudo about the size of a silver dollar—and ran her fingers over the stamped cross on the front. She threw it back in, and it clinked into the pile, landing next to a small gold cross with a few emeralds still embedded in it.

"This is worth a lot of money," Celeste said.

Luke shrugged. "Sure, but it's of no value to us. We can't keep it. Nor do we need it."

"Right. But it's not a relic or anything paranormal, and I was thinking maybe we could use it to help Jason."

Luke's brows tugged together. "I'm not sure. We're supposed to turn any additional treasure we bring back over to Dorian, even if it's not part of our main mission."

"Technically, we're supposed to report anything *we* bring back. But what if none of us brings this back?" Celeste raised her brows and looked at the others.

Morgan nodded. "You mean someone *other* than us?"

Luke pressed his lips together. "Now that you mention it, in all the excitement, it's hard to remember what we did find. The important thing is we found the relic. Who cares about anything else?"

"Right."

"I don't remember finding anything else." Gordy glanced up from the large cooler where he was repacking the remaining food.

"Me either." Buzz dropped his sleeping bag and duffel bag on the ground next to the other bags that had been placed there.

"I didn't see any box. I'm going to pack my cabin." Jolene turned toward her cabin.

"I'll help you." Matteo followed her.

Celeste flipped the lid shut on the box and slid it toward Jason. "I guess we better hurry and finish packing. I won't have room for anything extra."

"Me either," Luke said.

"I don't see anything extra," Jake added.

"Hey, wait." Jason had been standing back. He stepped up to the table. "I don't want to get you guys into trouble."

"Trouble? There's no trouble," Luke said. "We're the only ones that know what was found here. And all I remember finding is the relic. Anything else is fair game, just like it always has been for anyone who comes to hunt treasure on the island. Now we're going to finish packing up and then take this stuff to the boat. See you down there."

They all turned from the table and headed to their cabins.

Cal caught up with Celeste.

"So you decrypted the code on the rocks? How'd you do that?" He shoved his hands in his pockets and hunched his shoulders. "I mean, I've been working on it for days, and then one little hint from a ghost breaks the code?"

"Sort of." Celeste pulled the fortune out of her pocket and handed it to Cal. "Remember that day we went through the boxes?"

"Yeah."

"I found this in there. I kept it for you since you like old weird stuff like this, but it turns out it was actually the key to decrypt the code. And the message on the rocks was coordinates. Longitude and latitude."

"Not directions?" Cal asked.

"Nope. That's why it seemed shorter than it should be. Mirabella said that she was sure LeBlanc had deciphered the code. At first, I thought the clue Dorian got that set us off on this mission was the key, but Jolene ran that through the software, and we didn't get anything that made sense. Then I thought about that strange line at the end. *My fortune is resolved.* It always sounded awkward to me, and then I figured out why."

"It was a hint that the key was hidden inside a fortune cookie."

"Yep. Just so happened I had that fortune in my pocket still." Celeste shrugged it off as if it were down to luck, but now she knew it wasn't luck. It was her initial spell that had brought the fortune cookie to her.

"Well, I guess you solved it. You figured out where the relic was, and you retrieved it." Cal put his arm around her and squeezed her shoulders. "Don't you think that maybe my lessons on deciphering code are paying off just a little bit, though?"

"Oh, definitely." Celeste took his hand and led him into the cabin. Just before entering, she glanced over toward the cliff. No sign of Mirabella. Hopefully, she'd moved on with Constantine to wherever ghosts went. Pride rushed through Celeste. For once, she'd been instrumental in the success of their mission, and now both she and Mirabella could rest easy.

CHAPTER NINETEEN

Celeste snugged her jacket around her as she stepped off the boat onto the dock at Jason's marina. Behind her, Gordy, Buzz, Luke, Jake, and Cal were busy lugging their gear into the RV that Dorian had sent to meet them.

She watched Luke hand the relic over to Dorian. Dorian slipped it into a steel briefcase, which she snapped shut, spinning the cylinder locks on the front. Her eyes drifted out toward the dock where the Blackmoore sisters stood. She nodded at them before she slipped into the back of a black limousine and sped off.

"She never was one for small talk." Morgan came up behind Celeste. Her eyes trailed the back of the limo as it turned into the main road. She turned and thrust her chin toward the RV. "At least this time she sent us a comfortable ride."

Celeste hitched her backpack over one shoulder and started toward the RV. "Because she got what she wanted."

"Yeah, thanks to you. If it wasn't for you, we probably never would've found the relic. And Christian wouldn't be getting the medical treatment he needs."

Celeste's heart warmed at her sister's genuine praise. "Glad I could help."

She glanced over at the house to see Cal slipping something into Jason's hand. Behind them, Belladonna was busy rubbing her face against Christian's ankles. The little boy leaned forward, grasping the arm of his wheelchair with one hand while petting the cat with the other. He had a wide smile on his face.

Celeste's brows tugged together. "How did Belladonna get out of her crate?"

Morgan shook her head and took off at a jog after the cat. "I don't know. Sometimes I think she's more magical than any of us."

Christian looked up at her, and Celeste waved before continuing on to the RV. The cat sure did have a knack for appearing in impossible places and always just in the nick of time.

At the RV, Matteo and Jolene were engaged in a struggle with Jolene's duffel bag. Each of them held one side of the handle and was tugging it back and forth.

"I can carry my own duffel bag." Jolene glared at Matteo.

"I know you can carry it, but I'm offering to be a gentleman." Matteo's lips quirked up in a boyish grin.

"When I need a gentleman, I'll call for one." Jolene jerked the bag out of his hand.

"Come on, you guys. You don't need to have this power struggle anymore now that you're even," Celeste said.

Jolene screwed up her face. "Even?"

"Yeah, remember Matteo saved you, so neither of you owes the other. If you have something going on, it's all from the heart, not from any sense of duty." Celeste wondered if that was what Jolene had really been afraid of. That Matteo wasn't pursuing her because he really liked her, but because he felt that he owed her after she'd risked her life to save his.

"Who said one of us felt that the other owed them?" Jolene slid her eyes to Matteo.

"I never felt that way. It was always from the heart." He grinned down at her. "But now that we're even..."

"Oh no. I'm not gonna start doing your bidding just because you pulled me out of that cavern." Jolene hefted the bag up on her shoulder and nudged him with her arm. "But, if you're nice, I might let you sit with me."

"Sounds like a good start." Celeste slipped in between them and inconspicuously dropped half an acorn into each of their pockets. She'd charmed the acorn before they'd gotten on the boat. The two halves would be attracted to each other, and some of that energy would rub off on Matteo and Jolene. Not that the two of them needed magic to be attracted to each other, but Celeste figured Jolene could use a little push, just in case she couldn't see how right Matteo was for her.

Celeste stepped onto the RV with a light heart, certain the charm would work. After all, she was on a roll with her spells. She slipped into the corner of the banquette and put her backpack beside her. Cal came in the RV, sliding in next to her.

"What was that you gave to Jason?" Celeste asked.

"A list of people that might be in the market to buy old treasure. You know, in case he ever digs something up on that island."

"Right. I don't think there is any treasure there, though."

"Nah, me either. But one could hope." Cal winked.

The rest of them boarded the RV. Morgan struggled with the cat carrier, Belladonna inside, meowing very loudly. Luke swung up into the driver's seat. "Okay, everyone ready?"

"Yep. Let's roll."

As they drove off, Celeste waved out her window at Christian, who was smiling in his wheelchair. She settled into her seat with the satisfied feeling of a job well done. She couldn't have asked for a better outcome for this mission. Hopefully, the next one would turn out just as well.

THE END.

****

Sign up to join my email list to get all my latest release at the lowest possible price, plus as a benefit for signing up today, I will send you a copy of a new Leighann Dobbs book that hasn't been published anywhere...yet!
http://www.leighanndobbs.com/newsletter

Join my readers group on Facebook and get the inside scoop on my books -
https://www.facebook.com/groups/ldobbsreaders

If you want to receive a text message on your cell phone when I have a new release, text COZYMYSTERY to 88202 (sorry, this only works for US cell phones!)

Want more Blackmoore Sister's adventures? Buy the rest of the books in the series For Your Kindle:

Dead Wrong
Dead & Buried
Dead Tide
Buried Secrets
Deadly Intentions
A Grave Mistake
Spell Found
Fatal Fortune

Cozy Mysteries

Kate Diamond Mystery Adventures

***

Hidden Agemda (Book 1)

Ancient Hiss Story (Book 2)

Heist Society (Book 3)

Silver Hollow

Paranormal Cozy Mystery Series

***

A Spell of Trouble (Book 1)

Spell Disaster (Book 2)

Nothing to Croak About (Book 3)

Cry Wolf (Book 4)

Mooseamuck Island Cozy Mystery Series

* * *

A Zen For Murder

A Crabby Killer

A Treacherous Treasure

Mystic Notch

Cat Cozy Mystery Series

* * *

Ghostly Paws

A Spirited Tail

A Mew To A Kill

Paws and Effect

Probable Paws

Blackmoore Sisters

Cozy Mystery Series

* * *

Dead Wrong

Dead & Buried

Dead Tide

Buried Secrets

Deadly Intentions

A Grave Mistake

Spell Found

Fatal Fortune

Lexy Baker Cozy Mystery Series

* * *

Lexy Baker Cozy Mystery Series Boxed Set Vol 1 (Books 1-4)

Or buy the books separately:

Killer Cupcakes

Dying For Danish

Murder, Money and Marzipan

3 Bodies and a Biscotti

Brownies, Bodies & Bad Guys

Bake, Battle & Roll

Wedded Blintz

Scones, Skulls & Scams

Ice Cream Murder

Mummified Meringues

Brutal Brulee (Novella)

No Scone Unturned

Cream Puff Killer

Hazel Martin Historical Mystery Series

***

Murder at Lowry House (book 1)

Murder by Misunderstanding (book 2)

Lady Katherine Regency Mysteries

***

An Invitation to Murder (Book 1)

The Baffling Burglaries of Bath (Book 2)

Sam Mason Mysteries

(As L. A. Dobbs)

***

Telling Lies (Book 1)

Keeping Secrets (Book 2)

Exposing Truths (Book 3)

Betraying Trust (Book 4)

Romantic Comedy

***

Corporate Chaos Series

In Over Her Head (book 1)

Can't Stand the Heat (book 2)

What Goes Around Comes Around (book 3)

Contemporary Romance

***

Reluctant Romance

Sweet Romance (Written As Annie Dobbs)

Firefly Inn Series

***

Another Chance (Book 1)

Another Wish (Book 2)

Hometown Hearts Series

***

No Getting Over You (Book 1)

A Change of Heart (Book 2)

***

Sweetrock Sweet and Spicy Cowboy Romance

Some Like It Hot

Too Close For Comfort

Regency Romance

* * *

Scandals and Spies Series:

Kissing The Enemy

Deceiving the Duke

Tempting the Rival

Charming the Spy

Pursuing the Traitor

Captivating the Captain

The Unexpected Series:

An Unexpected Proposal

An Unexpected Passion

Dobbs Fancytales:

Dobbs Fancytales Boxed Set Collection

———

Western Historical Romance

***

Goldwater Creek Mail Order Brides:

Faith

American Mail Order Brides Series:

Chevonne: Bride of Oklahoma

————————————

Magical Romance with a Touch of Mystery

***

Something Magical

Curiously Enchanted

ROMANTIC SUSPENSE

WRITING AS LEE ANNE JONES:

***

The Rockford Security Series:

Deadly Betrayal (Book 1)

Fatal Games (Book 2)

Treacherous Seduction (Book 3)

Calculating Desires (Book 4)

Wicked Deception (Book 5)

A NOTE FROM THE AUTHOR

I hope you enjoyed reading this book as much as I enjoyed writing it. This is the eighth book in the Black-moore sisters mystery series and I have a whole bunch more planned!

The setting for this book series is based on one of my favorite places in the world - Ogunquit Maine. Of course, I changed some of the geography around to suit my story, and changed the name of the town to Noquitt but the basics are there. Anyone familiar with Ogunquit will recognize some of the landmarks I have in the book.

The house the sisters live in sits at the very end of Perkins Cove and I was always fascinated with it as a kid. Of course, back then it was a mysterious, creepy old house that was privately owned and I was dying to go in there. I'm sure it must have had an attic stuffed full of antiques just like in the book!

Today, it's been all modernized and updated—I think you can even rent it out for a summer vacation. In the book the house looks different and it's also set high up on a cliff (you'll see why in a later book) where in real life it's not. I've also made the house much older to suit my story.

Also, if you like this book, you might like my Mystic Notch series which is set in the White Mountains of New Hampshire and filled with magic and cats. You can find out more about this series on my website.

This book has been through many edits with several people and even some software programs, but since nothing is infallible (even the software programs) you might catch a spelling error or mistake and, if you do, I sure would appreciate it if you let me know - you can contact me at lee@leighanndobbs.com.

Oh, and I love to connect with my readers so please do visit me on facebook at http://www.facebook.com/leighanndobbsbooks or at my website http://www.leighanndobbs.com.

Want a free never-before-published novella from my Lexy Baker culinary mystery series? Go to: http://www.leighanndobbs.com/newsletter and enter your email address to signup - I promise never to share it and I only send emails every couple of weeks so I won't fill up your inbox.

ABOUT THE AUTHOR

Leighann Dobbs discovered her passion for writing after a twenty year career as a software engineer. She lives in New Hampshire with her husband Bruce, their trusty Chihuahua mix Mojo and beautiful rescue cat, Kitty. When she's not reading, gardening or selling antiques, she likes to write cozy mysteries and romances. Find out about her latest books and how to get discounts on them by signing up at:

http://www.leighanndobbs.com/newsletter

Connect with Leighann on Facebook:

http://facebook.com/leighanndobbsbooks

Join her private readers group on Facebook:

https://www.facebook.com/groups/ldobbsreaders/

Made in the USA
Columbia, SC
26 September 2023

23430587R00113